Another Claudia

books by Rose Franken

PLAYS:

ANOTHER LANGUAGE

MR. DOOLEY JR.

CLAUDIA: A PLAY

NOVELS:

PATTERN

TWICE-BORN

OF GREAT RICHES

CLAUDIA

CLAUDIA AND DAVID

THE BOOK OF CLAUDIA

ANOTHER CLAUDIA

Another Claudia

by

ROSE FRANKEN

FARRAR & RINEHART, INC.
NEW YORK   TORONTO

W

.F 8527a

121130

To My Son,
Lieutenant Paul Franken

Another Claudia

One

"WHAT'S NICER THAN WAKING UP IN THE MORNING and hearing your own lawn mower mowing your own lawn?" demanded Claudia sleepily.

David said he could think of lots of things nicer. Of course he might have meant Bobby trying to whistle or Majesty mooing, or even the clank of the milk pails as Edward carried them up the back porch from the barn. "However, we've no time to discuss it now," Claudia prudently decided.

She swung to the floor, and started rumpling up the other bed. "Too much; you're not an artist," David threw over his shoulder on his way to shave. "And anyway, don't think you're fooling Jane."

"I'm not doing it for Jane," said Claudia, "I'm doing it for myself—it makes me feel more refined to know both beds were slept in."

"I need my coffee," said David.

She followed him, and banged on the door. "Don't be in there all day! I have to get in too, I'm driving into town with you."

His eye appeared behind a cautious crack. "Why?"

"To see Hartley while he's still in the hospital."

Her faint edge of sanctity did not deceive him. "I know you well enough to know," said he, "that my brother's gall bladder isn't taking you into New York on a hot day."

"There's a sale of garden furniture," she admitted.

"Let it go until tomorrow."

"Sales don't go until tomorrow."

"Whether they do or they don't," he warned her darkly, "I have to be in the office at nine-thirty, and I'm not going to wait around for you."

She said, "Don't worry, you won't have to wait around for me."

She was lithe as a flea, ducking under his arm to wash her teeth, and bobbing her face in front of his while he was tying his tie.

"You're hell," he said gloomily. "I wish we had separate bathrooms."

"So do I," she agreed devoutly.

"Why don't you use the children's?"

"It's never the same."

"It doesn't have to be the same."

"Don't be so grumpy. I'm finished now.—How do I look?"

"All right," he said, going back to his tie.

"You don't so much as glance at me, and you say 'all right'—"

"I glanced at you."

"You didn't.—Button my top button, please."

He buttoned her top button.

"I don't think I like the spirit in which you do it," she remarked. "Anyone would think I don't know what." She picked up her gloves and purse. "And would you mind stopping dawdling? My sale begins at half past nine, and I'm not going to wait around for you."

She was off before he could speak his mind, but as luck would have it, she tripped on the stairs and made a great noise as she slid to the bottom. David rushed to the upper landing with his tie still untied. "Can't you look where you're going!" he bellowed with belated fury welling up in him. "I suppose you were taking two steps at a time in your usual fashion!"

"Two at a time, almost three," she corrected as pleasantly as she could through the pain that ripped her kneecap.

"Are you hurt?"

"No, I'm not hurt," she retorted.

"Serves you right if you busted a rib," he muttered.

"Well, I didn't bust a rib. Are you very disappointed?"

She was still hobbling when she entered the kitchen a few moments later. The kitchen was like Grand Central Station, with Bobby and Matthew under foot, and a waiting line outside the window. The Danes stood drooling over the smell of bacon, while Shakespeare sat upon the sill and pretended to be asleep. "Too high and mighty to be interested in food," Claudia jeered at him, and ran her thumbnail down the screen in front of his nose. He ignored her utterly, and after the way of cats, withdrew without withdrawing, and, amazingly, closed eyes that were already closed.

"No wonder he's not interested," Jane grimly offered, as she stirred the cereal. "I set the table on the terrace, as it's the first day warm enough, and he licked up all the butter."

"We're eating breakfast on the terrace like a picnic!" Bobby enlarged with much elation.

Claudia's heart sank. Jane had so recently succeeded Bertha that she had not yet had time to learn the singular ins and outs of the Naughton household. Bertha, for example, had known that it was practically wasted effort to open both beds at night. She had also known that in spite of having bought a farm, they made a point of discouraging weekend guests, and in addition were completely indifferent to hobby gardening, and all forms of outdoor eating.

"You might as well know it sooner or later—I want to have all my meals under cover, and I prefer my Sundays without company," David had defiantly made clear, even before they had moved out of New York.

Claudia had stared at him in unbelieving wonder. It was incredible luck that they should both be peculiar about the same things.

"And how do you feel about flowers?" he'd gone on, wanting to hear the worst.

"I love them," she'd confessed. "I hope you don't mind."

"I don't mind within limits," he'd grudgingly allowed. "Only don't go brooding over every bug and blight, and leap up mornings at five A.M. to weed."

"Don't be silly," she'd assured him, "I wouldn't leap at five A.M. in the morning to do anything. . . . And if I don't go to parent-teacher meetings for my children, why should I develop intelligentsia over a garden?"

David had seemed quietly and enormously satisfied at being wedded to such supreme normality. "Never let the simple life make you too simple," he had begged her.

"Nor too complicated," she'd amended. It had been a little like a second marriage vow.

This morning, however, as she stepped out onto the sunny terrace, dappled with the dizzy pattern of the maple tree, she wondered guiltily if they mightn't have been missing something in high-hatting Nature. The air was delicious, washed clean with dew, and filled to overflowing with the scent of fresh-cut grass. She took a great breath of it on the sly, holding it in her lungs and letting it out slowly. She was in the middle of a second breath when David dashed through the door, looking for his coffee like a madman. "What's the idea?" he demanded.

"Jane didn't know any better; she thought it

would be nice to have breakfast out of doors," Claudia apologized.

David's fountain pen gave him away as it lifted on his chest. "It's not bad," he acknowledged sheepishly. "What's the matter we don't do it all the time?"

"I wouldn't know," said Claudia.

It was not all sunshine and harmony, however, for Bluff and Bluster soon got wind that the scene of activities had shifted from the kitchen. Panting with enthusiasm and a desire to co-operate, they made a dash to the terrace, and ended up just short of knocking Matthew from his high chair.

"Hey!" David expostulated. "Who asked you to come?"

They sighed gustily in answer, and rested their chins on the table, and rolled their great sad eyes from plate to plate. "Move, please," said Jane, finding herself completely blocked against passing the scrambled eggs.

"They can't move," said Claudia. "They're nailed to the ground."

"They'll move," said David, with a good whack on each of their rumps.

Bluff must have had one of his odd reflexes on that particular spot of his rear, for he jumped a mile high and tipped over the cream pitcher.

"Think nothing of it, voilà service," said Claudia, and waved toward Shakespeare, who emerged from nowhere, and daintily made hay.

The Danes needed a little time to think it all out, but once they got the general idea, the puddle was as good as gone. Behinds in air, and elbows knock-kneed on the ground, they mopped it up with yards of sloshing tongue—and immediately it wasn't there.

Shakespeare was nobody's fool. He backed off in humps, his tail a swollen banner of hostilities. The Danes bared their savage teeth. Jane almost dropped the tray. "Oh, the poor cat!" she cried, not knowing that the shoe was on the other foot.

It was all over before it began. Shakespeare slapped their faces, and then molded himself into an orange square, and contemptuously went to sleep. Quaking, the dogs climbed into Claudia's lap and draped their endless paws across her. "My heroes," she embraced them. "Phew," she broke off. "You've been off with a skunk."

"I smell it, too!" Bobby shouted. "Phew! I smell it, too!" He held his nose and retched with realism, while Matthew applauded the performance by throwing his saucer in the air and screaming shrilly.

"This is a madhouse. Quiet down, both of you!" David ordered.

"You'd think, the way they act," said Claudia, "that a skunk was something to carry on about."

David lowered his paper. "Your mother is one of the few women who can take the smell of skunk completely in her stride," he commented with a degree of pride.

"I don't mind mice either," Claudia modestly reminded him.

"Your mother," continued David, removing a fly from his beloved coffee, "is a very remarkable woman."

"Is she?" Bobby queried in a subdued voice.

"She is," David stated with finality.

Claudia grew warm with pleasure. It was nice to know that David felt that way about her. "I'm a hell of a swell guy," she agreed complacently.

"You said a bad word!" Bobby announced, with his respect rising by leaps and bounds. "Oh, look!" he broke off, "what a beauty caterpillar!"

Claudia followed his enchanted gaze. The caterpillar had dropped from the maple tree, and was oozing its way across the table. A shudder ran down her spine. If there was one thing in the world she didn't like, it was caterpillars. "Take it away!" she squealed.

"But it's a beauty caterpillar," Bobby reiterated. He stroked it lovingly, and let it slither over his hand.

Claudia repressed another and more violent shudder. "There isn't any such expression as 'beauty caterpillar'," she rasped. "Now throw it away! Quick!"

Bobby lifted eyes that were direct and guileless. "Are you afraid of caterpillars?" he asked.

"Mama's not afraid of anything," David injected from behind his paper.

The flush of pleasure that had tinged Claudia's

cheeks deepened to a burning shame. She wanted to cry out, "You're wrong! I might not be afraid of lions or tigers, but I'd rather die than touch a caterpillar!"

"I'll let you hold it," Bobby suggested magnanimously.

Claudia pushed back her chair, knowing the nearest thing to physical panic that she had ever felt. "David, we have to leave, or we'll be late!" she cried in a smothered voice.

David glanced at his watch, and jumped to his feet. "Holly smokes, I should say so! . . . So long, pups. . . . Say, listen, Shakespeare, keep your fur to yourself next time. . . . Oh, Jane, try to find my pipe-scraper, will you?"

"That pipe-scraper again," said Claudia unsteadily. "Jane, please watch the children carefully."

"Yes, ma'am, I will. Don't worry."

"Daddy, look a minute. Isn't this a beauty caterpillar?"

David looked a minute. "Very handsome," he agreed.

"Better not play with it any more," said Jane. " 'Twill only hurt the poor thing. Let Jane put it on a bush for you."

Jane's a better man than I am, thought Claudia miserably, as she followed David to the car. She looked back to wave. A tree got in her way. David's fingers were brutal on her arm. "Good Lord, will you never learn to watch where you're going!" he upbraided her.

She disengaged herself from his uncivil grasp. "You can be the nastiest and the nicest man at the same time I ever saw," she said.

"That's my charm."

"You think you're charming?"

"Decidedly. Don't you?"

"I do not. . . . Would you like me to drive?"

"I would not."

He slid beneath the wheel. She settled herself beside him. They drove awhile in silence.

"How anyone could bump into a tree in broad daylight!" he suddenly burst out.

"I didn't bump into a tree, the tree bumped into me."

"You're going to kill yourself one of these days," he prophesied resignedly.

"A lot you'd care."

"I mightn't care, but you'll make a mess all over the place."

He was still harping on her ambulatory deficiencies, when he let her off on Fifth Avenue, opposite her sale. "Hurry up," he said, "while I watch you cross the street."

She said, "You don't have to watch me cross the street, thank you."

His hand shot through the car window and pulled her back to the curb. "Wait for the traffic light!" he cried hoarsely. "Or are you too good for traffic lights?"

"Much too good," she conceded amiably.

The sale, like most sales, was a masterpiece of exaggeration. The only thing that was exciting was a canopied chaise longue. A salesman came to life when he saw her looking at it, and plunged into immediate intimacy. "Isn't that a precious piece?" he burbled.

Claudia thanked God for David.

"And such marvelous value!" he went on. "Reduced to only a hundred and forty dollars!"

You flatter me, thought Claudia. Aloud she said, "Some other time."

He knew as well as she did, that their ways parted then and there, but he was the kind to believe in miracles, so he gave her his card. He said, "I'll be delighted to take care of you, Miss."

He had flattered her again by calling her "Miss". But then hardly anyone ever took her for a wife and mother, probably because she still had the figure of a bluefish, and her face, David always said, didn't have much sense to it. "Still I've gone through quite a lot," she'd said to him the other day, when they were talking of old times.

"Quite a lot," he'd agreed, "considering you've lived less than quarter of a century. And you take it like a gentleman," he'd added unexpectedly.

It had been the nicest compliment he'd ever paid her. She didn't fool herself, though. Actually, she knew that she wouldn't be worth two cents without him. She was a whole person only because she was married to him. His strength made her strong, and his wisdom made her knowing. If he'd only realize that she wasn't as perfect as he thought she was, she'd feel a little more honest in accepting his respect. Take this morning, for instance. She wondered what he'd say if he knew how things really stood between her and caterpillars. In a way, it was much easier to live with a man like Hartley, who had no contempts at all. Julia not only didn't like caterpillars, she didn't like dogs, yet Hartley continued to stay married to her. If it had been David, he'd have spanked her bottom, or gotten himself a divorce. But Hartley merely gave up his pair of pedigreed Dalmatians, and developed gall-bladder trouble instead.

He had to have it taken out eventually, and almost died of an entirely different ailment, which, Claudia gathered, was of a much more private nature. "That's what comes of playing the stock market," she pointed out to David, but David said it came from being married to Julia.

However, Hartley managed to pull through his various crises, and Claudia found him propped up on his pillows in his luxurious hospital room, looking like somebody else with his moustache shaved off and the open neck of his pajamas revealing a pale and vulnerable flabbiness. Pajamas always did wonders for David, but Hartley seemed rather pathetic in his gay silk stripes. People probably stopped looking nice in bed when they were over forty, Claudia decided.

Julia was with him, frightfully well-bred and stunning as usual, though not a bit pretty. She was sitting in a chair, with her hat and gloves on like company, and, like company, she was discussing inflation, and would the United States get into the war—which was silly, as of course it wouldn't.

"I hope you're right," said Hartley.

"War is for barbarians," Claudia asserted conclusively, gazing around the room for an interesting box. Unfortunately, however, Hartley was in the unremunerative stage of a long recuperation, and even the flowers were on their last legs.

"There's some crystallized fruits in the table drawer," Julia suggested, with a surprising flash of wit.

Claudia had no patience with crystallized fruits. They were neither one thing nor another, and stickier than they were worth. Nevertheless, she made the best of a bad bargain, and chose a promising affair wrapped elaborately in silver paper. It turned out to be nothing more than a dressed up prune.

"I knew it," she said bitterly. "There ought to be a law."

Hartley wanted to know a law about what.

"Prunes."

He couldn't quite get the connection, and Julia, who had apparently shot her wad of humor for the day, said that personally she found prunes extremely efficacious.

Claudia started to explain that there wasn't any fun in eating for efficacy, only it didn't seem worth the effort. She was really fond of Julia and Hartley— they were unfailingly generous on Christmas, birthdays and anniversaries—but they were difficult to talk to. She was glad when Dr. Rowland appeared at the door on his morning rounds, and interrupted an uninspired conversation about the children, but as luck would have it, he went into the same business all over again. He had brought Bobby and Matthew into the world—(at reduced rates, thanks to Julia)—and probably thought it his duty to enquire about them.

"And how's that clever young architect of yours?" he went on, smiling the successful kind of smile that had absolutely no smile in it.

"Oh, fine," said Claudia, a little wearily.

"And the rest of the family?"

"Fine," said Claudia, resisting the impulse to remind him that there wasn't any 'rest'.

"That's fine," said Dr. Rowland. He walked over to the bed and pulled back Hartley's pajama coat in a proprietary way and pushed his stomach around. He was a gynecologist, pure and simple, but having operated on Julia the year before, he now had a hand in Hartley for friendship's sake. "How do you feel?" he asked.

"Not too well," said Hartley.

"Fine," said Dr. Rowland vaguely, and somehow the conversation got back on to inflation.

"This is no place for me," Claudia decided. Inflation was as confusing as daylight saving time—she could never remember whether you added or subtracted. "I have to go," she said.

"Take the crystallized fruit with you," said Julia.

"Don't be silly," said Claudia.

She was glad to get out into the warm sunshine again, away from the thin, devastating odor of hospital disinfectant. She hurried to a drugstore to call David. Suppose, she thought with a moment of terror as she dialed the number, that the subtle magic between them had suddenly ceased to be? Suppose, like Julia and Hartley, they didn't have anything to talk about except current events?

His secretary was out to lunch. He answered the telephone himself. She always loved the way he said hello.

"Hello," she returned.

"Who's it?" (He knew perfectly well who it was.)

" 'S me," she said.

"Oh, 's you," he replied.

They'd have been nauseated if any two other grown people carried on like that, but with themselves it was a little like being in a car and not being able to smell your own brakes burning.

Before they knew it, the operator was asking for another nickel. Claudia scrabbled in her pocket-book. "Oh, operator, I haven't got it!" she discovered in dismay. "Can't you trust me for it?"

The operator had the soul of a spinster. "Kindly deposit an additional five cents," she insisted heartlessly.

"Oh God," said Claudia, distraught.

"Give me the number of the booth, I'll call you back," said David, being very capable. But just as he was going to do it, she found a nickel hiding in the folds of her handkerchief. She popped it in the slot. For a moment, the zang of the popping separated them. Her heart skipped until she heard his voice again.

"My wife's in New York," he mentioned evilly. "How about driving out to my farm in the country and spending the night with me? There's an extra bed, hardly ever been slept in."

"I can't. My children expect me home this evening. . . . Let's stop," she broke off. "This is getting really bad."

"It is," he admitted.

"How about lunch?"

"I thought you were shopping."

"I'm finished."

"What did you buy?"

"Nothing. Everything was too expensive. I decided to paint my old."

"Your old what?"

He could be stupid at times. "Old garden furniture, of course," she told him impatiently.

"Just a moment," he said, "if there's any painting to be done, I'll do it."

Resentment flared. "So you think I can't paint."

"No woman can paint," said he. "Are you having lunch with me, or aren't you?"

"Not if you think women can't paint. . . . I saw your brother, you might have the decency to ask how he was."

"He's all right."

"How do you know?"

"Well, isn't he?"

"Yes," she admitted. "I saw Julia, too," she added virtuously.

"It wasn't necessary to run around like a lunatic."

"I didn't run around like a lunatic, she was right in the room with him."

"Please deposit another nickel, Madam," the operator injected out of another clear sky.

"Oh dear," said Claudia, "I haven't got any more nickels, don't you remember?"

The receiver clicked warningly.

"David!" she cried, with a lost feeling, "Do you want to call me back?"

"No! Come on down, I'm hungry!"

"I'm starved too! I'll be there in ten minutes! Good-bye!"

"Good-bye!" he said.

Claudia hung up with a pleasant glow of having gotten in a couple of sentences over the operator's head. She opened the door of the booth and found a hostile-eyed man with a signet ring on his fourth finger, waiting to use the telephone. "I'm so sorry to have been so long," she told him happily.

She stopped at the tobacco counter on the way out and gave the clerk a sunny smile. "I want a cigar," she said. "Something for a dollar."

"We don't have any dollar cigars," said the clerk. "Fifty cents is the best we carry."

Her face fell. "Nothing better?"

"The fifty-cent one is a very nice smoke, Miss."

"Well, I should hope it would be," she rejoined brusquely. "That's a terrific amount of money to spend for one cigar. A woman could buy a pound of candy for fifty cents."

There was no doubt in his mind that he had made the sale, so he withdrew the box from the showcase. "How many do you want, Miss?"

"None," she said. "I want a dollar cigar."

He swallowed his Adam's apple and looked blank. He probably thinks I'm a moron, she thought cheerfully, as she left the store. She probably was, considering that David smoked a pipe. It didn't matter though. Twice in their marriage he had brought her orchids, explaining that although he knew she wasn't crazy about them, nothing less than an orchid could possibly express how he felt about her as a wife.

Now, by the same token, nothing less than a dollar cigar could possibly express how she felt about him as a husband.

Conveniently, there was a tobacco shop directly across the street. She headed toward it. The traffic light changed to red. With considerable conflict, she moved back to the curb, but after a few moments of impatient waiting, decided that it was stupid to waste half one's life in being cautious. Besides, she had promised to be at David's office in ten minutes. With a little ingenuity she could easily scoot between the cars, and if the policeman didn't like it, it would teach him to change his lights oftener.

She was about to step forth when a bright blue ball rolled across her foot. She picked it up and looked around to see where it had come from. A nice colored woman came puffing up, holding a little girl by the hand. The child wasn't much older than Matthew, but she could walk, and talk, and competently demanded the return of her property.

Her mother nudged her. "Selena, you say 'please' to the lady."

Selena opened her buttonhole of a mouth and piped out an obedient "please." Claudia had a weakness for little colored babies, especially when they were round and shiny and bowlegged. It would be a nice change in the family to have one, she thought.

She was considering the effect upon David and the community, when she became aware that Selena had

bounced the ball toward her in an overture of friendship. It wasn't a good bouncer, and rolled sideways
into the gutter. Selena pulled free of her mother's
hand, and darted after it. It was the only thing that
Claudia remembered—the way Selena's mother
screamed, and wheels that filled the universe.

There were faces staring down at her. "Stand
back!" a voice shouted. "Give her air!"

"Something must have happened," Claudia concluded. She wondered what, but her head ached too
much to try to find out. It ached all over her body.
It was an effort to keep her eyes open. She dropped
back into a comfortable darkness.

"Can you remember your name, lady?" the voice
asked from a long way off.

She didn't feel like talking or she would have given
him a piece of her mind. Why on earth shouldn't she
be able to remember her name? "Mrs. David Naughton," she replied shortly.

"And now, Mrs. Naughton, can you tell me your
address?" the voice continued.

It must have been a case of sheer mesmerism, because her brain balked at that point, and she couldn't
for the life of her remember where she lived. If there
was one thing she dreaded, it was losing her memory.
Her eyes flew open in panic. It was an additional
shock to find the traffic policeman bending over her.
Traffic policemen were reminiscent of speeding, or

forgetting her license. "I didn't do anything," she forestalled him hastily.

"No, lady, you didn't do anything," he agreed, quite gently. "There's been an accident."

"An accident?" She tried to sit up. Accidents never failed to fill her with the terror of something happening to the children or to David. "Was anybody hurt?" she asked, with the strength going out of her.

"Nobody was hurt but you, lady. You ran out in the street, and a car knocked you down."

It was only then that she realized that she was lying flat on the opposite sidewalk, surrounded by gaping onlookers. She was mortified. It was a picture that David had painted a hundred times, and life wouldn't be worth living if he found out about it. "Please help me to get up," she implored the policeman, "I'm not hurt, really I'm not!"

"Yes you are, lady," he contradicted firmly. "You just lie quiet until the doctor comes."

"But I don't need a doctor!" she protested. To prove it, she struggled to her feet. She could scarcely stand. The pain that had ripped her kneecap when she'd fallen down the stairs this morning was nothing compared to the way she felt now. I must have broken all my important bones," she thought in dismay. "David will be simply furious."

The policeman's hand was kindly on her shoulder. "You better let me help you into the tobacco shop," he advised.

"No, thank you," she returned politely, "I don't think I'll stop to buy a cigar now."

After a moment of blankness, he evidently decided that she was trying to be funny, and he gave a guffaw of laughter. It was the perfect moment to make her exit. She timed it exactly, pushing her way through the crowd to hail a taxi. She climbed painfully into it. A couple of women stared after her. "Look, she's not even hurt," she heard one of them exclaim in disappointment.

"Who says I'm not," she retorted under her breath. She leaned back against the seat, giddy with the agony of moving. "Hurry, driver. Please!" she gasped.

He was an affable taxi driver, with several moles on his face, and friendly as an uncle. "I'll hurry, Miss, if you tell me where you want to go," he answered, reasonably enough.

She gave him the address of David's office, which she was grateful to find on the tip of her tongue. I'm lucky I didn't get a good case of amnesia out of this, she reflected. That would have been all David needed to make him crow.

The driver dropped his flag and started off. "Pretty bad accident back there," he remarked. "Woman and child got knocked down by a car."

Claudia's blood froze as it all flooded back to her—the blue ball, and the little colored girl, and the mother's screams. She had to wet her lips before she could speak. "The child—did anything happen to it?"

"Child's all right, child wasn't hurt at all."

"Oh, thank heaven," she cried, thinking of Matthew.

"Woman was killed though," the driver continued laconically.

"Oh, no!"

"Sure thing. Stretched out back there on the sidewalk, dead as a door nail," he enlarged with gusto.

"It's strange I didn't see her," Claudia exclaimed. "I was stretched out on the sidewalk myself," she was about to add, when a thought occurred to her. "Was she a nice stout colored woman?"

The taxi driver snorted. "Nothing colored about her. White as you are. Just about your age, too."

"Oh," said Claudia, "I see."

There was a small pause. She cleared her throat. "Are you sure she's dead?" she enquired meekly.

The scream of an ambulance sufficed for answer. "Hear for yourself," said he.

She had the grace to blush. It must have cost the city a pretty penny to send an ambulance to fetch a corpse that wasn't there. She looked out of the window to make sure she wasn't being followed. "I wish you'd go a little faster," she urged him.

It was a relief when the cab drew to a stop in front of the familiar facade of David's office building. She swam through the revolving door, only to collide with Roger Killian, who was coming out. He was on his way, he said, for a treatment—which might have meant anything from a high colonic to a session with an Indian swami. Roger wasn't running over with masculinity, and he had a great deal of trouble with his digestion; but he was a fine architect and David's senior partner, so Claudia forced herself to stop for a little chat with him on the subject of no rain, and wasn't it perfectly dreadful for the lawns. Roger had a beautiful lawn and lovely gardens, and he was very particular about the weather.

Somebody else I know is just like him, but I can't for the life of me think who, she pondered. It was a fretful thing not to be able to remember, especially with the big lump on the back of her head a painful reminder that amnesia might be curled up inside of it, ready to pounce at any moment.

She could hardly wait to crawl into the haven of David's arms. He was standing by his desk, waiting for her. She managed a watery smile. "Hello," she said as nonchalantly as her throbbing nerves would permit.

It was apparently the worst opening she could have chosen. Too late, she realized that he, too, was in a state of nerves. He was also hungry. He thrust his wrist watch under her nose. "Two o'clock and no lunch!" he greeted her.

Lunch. When he heard about the ambulance, he wouldn't be thinking about lunch. She sank down in a chair and closed her eyes. "You're in a vile temper," she observed faintly.

"Vile temper!" he echoed, "why shouldn't I be in a vile temper! You say you'll be here in ten minutes, and an hour later you calmly march in!"

He was no less than loutish as he stood glowering down at her. She started to tell him that by the very skin of his teeth he wasn't a widower, but self-pity overcame her. "Feel," she gulped, and guided his unfriendly hand to the bump on her head.

"Where did that come from?" he demanded suspiciously, as if she'd stolen it off a beggar.

"I was almost killed!" she blurted out, "and you say I calmly walk in!"

"You were almost killed," he repeated ominously. "And may I ask how you were almost killed?"

An hour ago, over the telephone, he had been a sweet and clownish lover. Now he was a male with an empty stomach, a husband with a grievance. "Please don't glare at me like that!" she cried with hysteria mounting up in her. "I didn't do anything! Stop putting me in the wrong!"

His lips went into a straight line. "How did you almost get killed?" he reiterated.

"I fell down."

"Oh. So you fell down again."

It was low of him to slip in the word "again", for it changed the complexion of the episode, and started her off with a handicap. "I didn't exactly fall down," she attempted to explain.

"You didn't *exactly* fall down." He grabbed the

words out of her mouth before she could go any further, and twisted them in pure malice. "Then what did you do, may I ask, if you didn't 'exactly' fall down?"

"If you'll only keep quiet, I'll tell you the whole thing in a nutshell—"

"Nutshell is right," he injected.

Her nerves exploded in a single violent outburst. "I had an accident! I was run over! Now are you satisfied?"

"Completely," said he. "I always knew it would happen."

She controlled the desire to hit him. It was necessary for him to understand about the little colored girl. "Look," she started afresh, "I wanted to cross the street to buy you a cigar—"

"What the hell do I want with a cigar!" he broke in.

"Shut up!" she flung at him. "If you don't shut up, I won't say another word!"

He said that there was no need for her to say another word. "Next time," he said, "you'll wait for the lights to change. I have no sympathy for you."

"But the traffic light was red!" she expostulated. "I mean green! I mean it was whatever color it was supposed to be! I waited for it purposely!"

He smiled. "And a car came right up on the sidewalk, I suppose."

"You're impossible! You don't want to understand!" She began to cry. For an instant he looked as if he were going to take her in his arms, but instead he asked her gruffly where she'd hurt herself.

"All over," she sobbed. "And my last good pair of stockings is ruined!"

He looked down and for the first time saw the angry bruises through the torn mesh of her hose. With no comment whatsoever, he turned on his heel and went into Roger's office. She knew what he was after—Roger always kept bandages and tape in case of an emergency. She didn't, however, expect the iodine. "Hey, don't! That's going to hurt!" she cried out in Bobby's voice.

"Shut up!" he said briefly, rolling down her stockings.

"Don't you tell me to shut up!" she flared.

"Have you a monopoly on the expression?"

He put iodine on her forehead, too, where a stray bruise was belatedly swelling up. He smeared it on with relish, as if he were pointing a moral. She was tongue-tied with the smart of it, and numb with outrage at the way he was treating her. "Even a criminal," she said shakingly, "has a right to explain—"

"I don't need any explanation. You admit you were almost run over. That's enough."

She beat the air in frustration. "At least let me explain! You haven't any idea how it happened!"

"Oh, yes, I have," he returned smugly. "You didn't bump into a tree, a tree bumped into you."

Her pride would permit her to go no further. "Think what you want, and go to hell!" she shouted at him.

From that point on it became involved, because David didn't like to be told to go to hell, and besides, he was convinced that his ill-humor was justified by the great and abiding love he held for her. He didn't say it, but she knew how his mind functioned. "Deep and abiding love my hat," she vowed viciously. "I wouldn't explain now, if he got down on his hands and knees and begged me. What's more, I'm glad I didn't waste a dollar on a cigar for him."

They left for home almost immediately. "You'd better eat something," he said ungraciously, as they passed a sea-food restaurant on the road. Under ordinary circumstances, they would both have ordered lobster, and had a very good time. But David said he wanted only a cup of coffee, and Claudia constrained herself to the same, even though she could have managed a sandwich. It was worth the sacrifice, however, for he looked really worried for the first time, and muttered something about seeing a doctor.

"I don't need a doctor, thank you," she returned icily.

"No, you need a keeper," he retorted with a great deal of venom and very little brilliance.

They had no further conversation for the remainder of the trip. Claudia kept on trying to think whom

Roger had reminded her of, and David smoked one cigarette after another without smoking them. He drove like a lunatic—a skillful, even a careful lunatic, she had to admit—and vented his bad temper on innocent fellow motorists, mostly women.

They drew up at their white gate much earlier than usual. Bobby came running out to meet them. "Mother's got a lump on her forehead!" he noticed at once.

"I got it in New York, they're wearing lumps," said Claudia, trying to pretend that she and David were the best of friends. But David didn't have the decency to co-operate. "Your mother," he announced malevolently, "makes a profession of falling down. She thinks it's cute."

Bobby looked a little startled. The words had a familiar ring, and yet they were different. He drifted off to the homey refuge of the kitchen.

"That's right, give the child a neurosis," Claudia cried. "Let him see that his mother and father are unhappy together."

The ghost of a smile pulled at the corners of David's lips, and if she had given one small answering flicker, their quarrel would have been as good as over. But once again her pride reared up on its hind legs. She turned her back on him and walked laboriously up the stairs, putting in an extra stagger for good measure.

He followed her. "Where are you going?"

"To bed," she said.

He knew she had to be practically dead to go to bed, but he disguised his concern with a growl. "Any pain any place?"

"I'm quite all right," she answered him off the top of her voice.

"You look all right," he muttered. "You look simply blooming."

He stamped off into the bathroom. When he returned she was already in her nightgown, turning down her blankets. She didn't feel in the least like going to bed. She was merely doing it to punish him for being a boor.

The joke was on her, however, for, wonders of wonders, she went right to sleep the minute her head touched the pillows. This is very odd, she thought, as she felt herself drift off into space. Nothing short of an appendix or a baby had ever before induced her to take a nap in broad daylight. She was vaguely conscious that David crept to the door every now and again to look at her, and she had a sense, as twilight deepened in the room, that Jane tiptoed to the threshold with a tray, and then tiptoed out again. Still, she couldn't rouse to talk to them, she could only go on sleeping in great hungry gulps.

When she opened her eyes it was morning. Her head, thank the Lord, was as clear as a bell, and she remembered at once whom Roger had reminded her of. "Ass, the salesman who sold me my garden furniture!" she said aloud.

David leaped out of his bed and hurried to her side. He regarded her with anxiety and laid his hand on her forehead. "I thought you didn't buy any garden furniture," he recalled gently to her memory.

"I didn't," she said. "But he reminded me of Roger anyway."

David thought about it. "Very possible," he nodded.

They smiled at each other. Everything was just the way it had always been between them. "You crazy loon," he said. "Let's see your legs."

She waved him away. "We're not quite that good friends yet. Let's have a mirror."

He brought her the hand glass. She sat up and looked at herself. "I'm a sight," she remarked with pride. "That lump is as big as an egg, almost."

"It's as big as a melon," he topped it, generously.

It was a truce. Now was the perfect time to clear up their quarrel. The honorable thing to do was to confess that she had really had every intention of crossing through a red traffic light yesterday, but hadn't actually done so because she had somehow gotten mixed up with a little colored girl and a blue ball. She didn't have a very straight picture of what had happened after that, but it wasn't important, anyway. Nothing seemed to matter except that David's arms were around her and he was scolding her against her ear for making his life a hell on earth. It was too bad it wasn't Sunday.

As it was, they were late for breakfast, just with talking. Jane was surprised to see that Claudia was up.

"You should have stayed right in bed, Mrs. Naughton. 'Twould have been no trouble," she said, "to bring you a tray."

"What would I do with a tray?" said Claudia. Except for a few little twinges here and there, she was as good as new, and the coffee smelled divine.

It was another lovely June morning, with pure white clouds in a pale blue sky. Jane, however, had callously set the table in the dining room. The dogs stared in through the windows, liquid with desire, but she turned her back on them. "Jane's cured," Claudia whispered to David.

"Cured of what?" asked Bobby.

"Cured," said David from behind his newspaper, "of the uncomfortable complications of advanced simplicity."

Bobby looked frustrated. The telephone rang. "I'm going to answer it," he retaliated.

David yanked him back by the seat of his pants. "No you don't," said he.

"Oh, let him answer this once," Claudia interceded. "It can't be anybody good this hour of the morning."

"How do you know it's not anybody good?" David argued. "Maybe it's the hospital. Maybe Hartley's taken a turn for the worse."

"At least look worried about it!" she reproved him.

"Why? We all have to die."

Claudia winced. "It's not human to be so detached; I could kick you when you talk like that!"

"You've no philosophy," he said amiably, as he helped himself to another piece of toast.

"What would I do with it if I had it?" she wanted to know. "Philosophy is something you get when you haven't got anything else.—And don't make such a noise chewing. I'm trying to listen who's on the telephone."

"I'd like to see you chew toast any quieter," he challenged.

She selected a piece and consumed it with an ostentatious lack of audibility. David dipped a teaspoon into his glass of water, and aimed precisely. Claudia's lips went into a straight line. She wiped her eye with one hand, and with the other picked up her own glass of water. "Better not," said David levelly, reaching for the pitcher.

They remained frozen for an instant, measuring the length of each other's intentions. It became a point of moral obligation for Claudia to throw the contents of her glass. David smiled pleasantly and threw the contents of the pitcher. Dripping, they regarded each other with respect. The incident was an emotional catharsis they had not known they needed until that moment.

Bobby came back. His face lit up as he noticed the prevailing dampness. "What happened?" he inquired with a lively interest.

Claudia decided that it would be poor judgment to set an example that would only backfire on her rugs and draperies. She fenced for time. "What do you mean, what happened?"

"You're all wet," said Bobby delightedly.

David caught the ball of evasion in Claudia's eye and neatly tossed it back. "All wet?" he echoed, in mild astonishment. "What are you talking about?"

"And who was on the wire?" Claudia demanded.

Bobby wavered between thwarted curiosity and importance. He succumbed to the latter. "Aunt Julia," he reported pompously. "She wants to talk to Daddy. In a hurry."

Claudia was appalled. "Now see what you've done," she cried accusingly. "You've wished a relapse on your brother!"

"Nonsense," said David. Nevertheless, he seemed a little upset and lost no time in getting to the telephone. Claudia jumped up to follow him.

"Maybe Uncle Hartley's dead," Bobby remarked, taking what comfort he could out of an alternate excitement.

"That's a nice way to talk." She hesitated at the

door, full of apprehension. "Did Aunt Julia sound that way?"

"What way?" asked Bobby.

The conversation was becoming too tenuous for clarity. "Never mind," she said.

"She did though," Bobby offered sagely.

"Did what?"

"Sound as if Uncle Hartley was dead."

Claudia frowned. "That's naughty."

"It's not," he defended. "She was very excited." A thought occurred to him. "Would it make you cry if Uncle Hartley died?" he asked her soberly.

"I'd feel pretty awful," she acknowledged. "Finish your cereal."

"But would you cry?" he insisted. "I hate it if you cry!" he added passionately.

She realized suddenly that the safety and completeness of his universe depended solely upon her own serenity. She turned back and put her arms around him. "Mothers never cry," she promised him.

"Would Daddy?" he continued anxiously. "Cry?"

She was in the act of assuring him that fathers were equally impregnable, when David rushed into the room and gave the lie to her contention. Whatever piece of news Julia had imparted over the telephone had destroyed his customary equilibrium.

"Where's the newspaper!" he shouted.

"For goodness sake," said Claudia. "What's the matter? Why?"

"Never mind, why! What'd I do with it, where is it?"

"Here it is," said Bobby, "on the floor."

"I suppose the damned old stock market fell again," Claudia concluded in disgust. Julia played the market too, and it was the only point on which she and David were really intimate. "Don't come to me for sympathy," she went on coldly. "I've begged you to keep out of it."

She might have been the wind blowing for all he paid attention to her. He found what he was looking for—some modest little item tucked away in the second section—and spanked the paper into shape. "A young woman," he read aloud, "who gave her name as Mrs. David Naughton, saved a child from the wheels of a truck yesterday, and disappeared into the crowd that rapidly gathered at the scene of the accident—"

Bobby choked on his cereal. "That's Mother!" he bleated.

"For goodness sake," said Claudia again.

David was half an hour late in starting for the office, for the phone kept ringing like mad, and before breakfast was over, the novelty had worn off even for Bobby, and they had to beg him to answer it.

"I never dreamed so many people read the newspaper all the way through," marveled Claudia, who rarely did more than glance at the headlines and the sales, and skip through the death notices, just in case she happened to know someone.

"Do you think everybody's an ignoramus like you are?" David demanded. "There happens to be a war going on in Europe."

"I know," she said, perfunctorily. It was difficult to think of a war in Europe with the sun shining in Connecticut, and the children well, and David proud enough to burst. He didn't let her know it, of course. He just gave her a whack on the backside and told her the next time she ran around New York saving lives, he'd wring her neck. "Your mother," he remarked to Bobby with rich irony, "is a hero. But she was too proud to tell anyone about it."

Bobby gave a hoot of approval. This was getting to be like old times. "My mother's a hero!" he echoed without awe.

Claudia was relieved at the way they took it. She would have hated it if they had made a fuss over her, particularly since she had the uncomfortable conviction that fear had a great deal to do with courage. You couldn't have one without the other, and the only thing in the world she wasn't afraid of was anything happening to herself.

"I'm really the worst coward that ever lived," she confessed to David, as she walked with him to the gate. She wanted to say, "If I ever lost you or the children, I couldn't go on living." But her throat closed against the words, she could not bring herself to voice them. She mumbled instead, "I'm afraid of caterpillars."

"You ought to be ashamed of yourself," said he.

"You're right," she said. She hugged his arm, rejoicing because it was so strong and hard and real against her breast. "I wish it were tonight," she murmured.

"So do I," he answered huskily.

He kissed her, and climbed into the car. She stood there, looking after him, long after he had disappeared down the road. Her heart was full of peace.

Two

DAVID WAS WORRIED. HE WOULDN'T ADMIT IT, BUT Claudia noticed how he wasn't interested in food all at once, and the way he'd scratch his head in bed, before he finally fell asleep. One night it got to be half past twelve, and he hadn't closed his eyes. She sat up and put on the lamp. "Look here," she said, "people scratch their heads for two reasons, and the other one's nerves."

He went through all the motions of having been ruthlessly wakened from deep slumber. "Don't lie," said Claudia. "What's bothering you?"

"Nothing. Turn around and go to sleep."

"I can't," she complained. "It's contagious. You've got me scratching too. I itch all over."

"Can I help it if you have no strength of character?"

"Something's worrying you," she maintained, stubbornly. A thought laid icy hands against her heart. He had not been looking well the past few weeks. "David, you're not ill, are you?" she whispered.

"You're crazy," he said.

Quickly she knocked on wood to propitiate Fate against his arrogance.

"Knocking wood is the distinctly middle-aged mark of a fat lady with a bust," he pointed out severely.

"Not at all," said she. "It's the artist in me. All artistic natures are superstitious. . . . Listen," she reverted, "you might as well tell me sooner or later."

"Tell you what?"

"Why you're acting this way. It's no pleasure to live with a man who won't eat."

David's lips twisted. "That's a funny one," said he.

"Is it another woman?" she persisted.

He began to clown, turning his head away in abject guilt.

"Don't be silly," she said. She pulled his face toward her again and scrutinized him closely, tracing with her finger tip new lines that had come around his lips. "I know," she said with finality. "It's that stock market. Margin again."

He bridled at that. "No, Miss Smarty, it's not 'margin again'. But I had to sell some securities at a loss," he admitted.

"Why?"

"I needed the cash."

"What for?"

"Forget it. It's my job to worry about finances, not yours."

"Since when? In this family we do the worrying together. . . . Are we awfully broke or just a little?"

He measured out half a yard or so with his hands.

"I could kill you," said Claudia.

He sat up and reached for a cigarette. "All right," he said shortly. "You asked for it. I borrowed a thousand dollars yesterday."

"In addition to the securities you sold?" she asked over the slight shock that tightened her throat.

"Yes. I had to bolster the business account."

"Oh. Who'd you borrow it from?"

"You. I drew it out of the savings bank."

She laughed aloud with relief. "You idiot, that was money you gave me for birthdays and things."

"Nevertheless it was yours."

"But I thought it was all used up on my appendix and Bobby's concussion last winter?"

"No," he said dryly. "I treated you to those. So far I've been able to support my family on what I earn."

" 'Support my family'," she jeered. "You sound like a dime novel."

"It's the male in me," he said ironically.

"Yes, and there comes a time in every man's life, when that's what's wrong with him."

He regarded her quizzically. "What do you mean?"

"I mean, stop taking your masculinity so seriously.

It's false pride to think that just because you wear pants you have to support a woman in luxury. By rights I ought to support myself."

She saw his jaw tighten, and she realized at once that she had made a wrong approach. "Only I'm not the type to earn my own living," she amended, and inwardly smiled to see his face relax. "Come on," he said, "let's put the light out and get some rest." In a few moments, he was off to sleep. Men aren't very complex, thought Claudia.

She lay awake for a long while, thinking. Wisdom came to her like some gracious visitor; she knew that she had to mother not two children, but three, and of these three David was the youngest, and the most in need of her. What was troubling him was more than a question of money, it was a sickness of soul eating deep into him. This that he was going through now was his own private defeat and confusion.

It would have been easy to let Jane go, and have soup meat instead of steak, but at a time like this, a man didn't need a virtuous wife to punctuate his deficiencies; he needed a good mistress to reinforce his ego. He didn't need forbearance; he needed the objective bickering of two people living under the same roof, to preserve his health and sanity.

Secretly, however, she resolved to embark without delay upon a regime of strictest economy. She spoke to Jane about it the next day. Jane was sweet. She had her hands full enough as it was, but she offered to do the sheets at home. In return, Claudia insisted on taking over the upstairs housework. Jane tried to talk her out of it, for she knew she wouldn't have an easy moment while she heard Claudia flying around overhead. Jane was a fool about dust, and corners, and taking all the covers off a bed before she made it, and sometimes Claudia found it difficult to meet her clear, searching gaze. But she couldn't be bothered by pangs of conscience when there was hay to get in, and no money to waste on extra day labor. "You don't have to bother about the truck garden," she told Edward, knowing perfectly well that she wouldn't be able to look a string bean in the face before the month was over.

Nevertheless her spirit held up gallantly through these busy days, although her nails broke down one by one. "I can't live with me another minute," she decided one morning, and telephoned the village beauty shop for a manicure appointment.

As always, she couldn't budge without Shakespeare and the dogs and Bobby at her heels. She might have been some kind of human magnet, the way they drifted after her, and congealed in solid mass, against the rear wheels of the station wagon as she backed from the garage. "All right, I'll run over the whole kit and kaboodle of you," she threatened.

The Danes didn't budge, knowing it for an idle threat, knowing it would hurt the car far more than it would hurt them. But Shakespeare, perversely, dissolved beneath the bumpers, and Bobby hopped, for safety, on the running board. "Which makes everything a lot easier," Claudia commented. "Get off, please."

"I won't fall," Bobby promised. He loved to ride on the running board. It gave him a sense of hazard, forbidden except for moments of parental leniency. "Don't ever try it with anybody but Mother or Daddy," Claudia frequently impressed upon him. "And better only with Daddy," David would inject. He refused to admit that she was a good driver, whereas she really was, except in backing, when she was apt to forget that the wheels turned in the opposite direction from the way she steered.

This morning, because of so much to-do around her, she found herself more than ever confused by this annoying contradiction of movement.

"You smashed into something," Bobby mentioned helpfully.

She climbed out of the car to investigate the damage. "Oh, dear," she said, and wondered how anything so substantial as a garage door could seem to be hanging by a thread.

Edward heard the crash from the barn, and came hurrying out to see what had happened. His ruddy Vermont color returned when he discovered that it was only a door. "Can you fix it?" Claudia anxiously besought him.

Edward was good at livestock, and he knew his

crops, but he was no magician. "I'm afraid I'll have to order some new lumber," he said.

"Oh, dear," said Claudia again. It was her second door that summer, and it was only July, which was just playing into David's hands. "I suppose we couldn't get it on before Mr. Naughton comes home?" she suggested shamelessly.

Edward shook his head. "Lumber yard won't deliver until tomorrow," he said.

Dejected, she started to climb back into the car. The dogs were too quick for her. They jostled past her and poured into the rear seat, where they planted themselves with a complete relaxation of tongue and saliva. Claudia knew from past experience that they would continue to slobber down her neck, but she also knew that it would take no less than dynamite to dislodge them.

"If the dogs go, I want to go too," Bobby declared.

"Nonsense. You'd be bored to death while I was getting my manicure. . . . When's the last time you brushed your teeth?"

He was not at all disturbed by the *non sequitur*. "Before breakfast," he replied.

"Which breakfast?"

"This morning. You can feel my toothbrush," he offered magnanimously.

"Thanks. Run up and brush them again to make sure."

"Then can I go with you?"

"No."

"But I have to buy something."

"What?"

He was vague about it, but Claudia finally uncovered the fact that he had seven cents in his pocket that needed spending. "I have to get a box of cigarettes for Daddy's birthday," he said.

"Daddy's birthday was last month, and anyway a box of cigarettes costs a lot more than seven cents," she disillusioned him.

"I can borrow the rest."

"Can you? Who from?"

"From you," he said.

"Ha, ha," said Claudia. "Ever hear of a church mouse?"

Apparently he hadn't. He remembered the town mouse and the country mouse, but he'd never met up with a church mouse. "Never mind," she said, "run help Edward with the chores."

It was a shabby trick to play on Edward, but since Bobby wasn't old enough to go out and sell newspapers, there was nothing to be gained by explaining that the family exchequer was much the worse for a hard winter's wear. It was funny how for years she hadn't given a thought to money. She had always considered it slightly vulgar when people bragged about having it, or not having it, but suddenly she was beginning to understand how, with a little swinging of the pendulum one way or the other, it could become the controlling factor of one's daily existence. A new garage door, for example, ceased to be merely a feather in David's cap. It was a two weeks' grocery bill, a session with the dentist, a row of shrubs for the garden wall.

Her spirit was low as she drove off. Jane and Matthew were waiting at the front gate to flag her as she turned out of the driveway.

"Please bring me a half pound of bacon," said Jane. "And at the same time you could ask the butcher for some nice bones for soup. He should give you them for nothing," she instructed firmly. "You want them for the dogs."

It was apparently the immemorial custom of cooks to think that owning a big dog paid off a sort of life annuity for soup. "I haven't the face, the butcher's on to us," Claudia objected. "Moreover, it's not honorable."

Jane looked righteous. "I don't see why it's not," she argued. "I always let them have the bones afterwards, and they're that much more tasty for having been with soup greens."

"I like soup," Matthew unexpectedly remarked.

"Well, don't talk about it," said Claudia. She glanced guiltily at Bluff and Bluster, but they weren't listening. They sat gazing into space, thinking deeply of nothing at all—so deeply in fact, that when she started the car, they lurched forward in a dead weight across her shoulders, and remained that way as she rolled along the countryside. "This is charming," she said bitterly.

A mile or so along, she slowed down to look at the house that David was building for Elizabeth Van Doren. David didn't like to build houses—he wasn't that kind of architect—but Elizabeth was Roger's cousin, so he was doing it as a favor. Besides he liked Elizabeth, and so did Claudia. It was going to be nice to have her for a neighbor. Elizabeth was their own kind. Somehow, in spite of the years that they had lived in Eastbrook, they were still city people as far as the natives were concerned. Even a Grange meeting once a month couldn't bridge the essential difference between New England and New York.

She was always lured by houses in the making. She drew to a full stop, taking an envious pleasure in the skeleton bay windows, and broad high corridors —architectural liberties that had no place in their salt-box cottage. Still, for all its spacious luxury, there wasn't much joy in building a home without a husband. A widow is the saddest thing on earth, thought Claudia. Sometimes she wondered how Elizabeth, so little older than herself, could move through the days with such quietude and acceptance. I couldn't, she brooded, as she stared at the gleaming empty bricks. I could never begin life over again all by myself.

She shuddered at the very thought, and stepped

on the gas. Ten minutes later she slid up against the curbing in front of GLORIANNA'S BEAUTY SHOPPE. Nancy Riddle's oppressively new and shiny station wagon was parked there too, with Nancy's liveried chauffeur and two fat cocker spaniels waiting patiently within. "There's something wrong with this picture," Claudia decided, as she rolled up the windows against four hundred pounds of dogflesh. "The rich keep cockers, and the poor keep Danes." She paused to look at them from the sidewalk. They had already misted the glass with their lolling tongues and rivulets were running down the panes. "Leaky, but angelic," she summarized, with a little lump of pure affection rising up in her. She waved to them, and they nearly waved back at her.

Glorianna's shop was sandwiched between Eastbrook's single drugstore and a gift emporium. It was small and modest, and exuded a warm smell of fresh paint and brilliantine. Claudia noticed at once that everything had been done over since her last visit. There was shiny brown linoleum on the floor, and the woodwork was a cheery yellow instead of the old lackadaisical green. There was a new drying machine too, and under it sat Nancy, looking all her age, with her pinkish hair held flat beneath a dun-colored veil, and wads of cotton sprouting out from above each ear. "Hello!" she yelled when Claudia came in. "I've been meaning to telephone you!" She probably thought she was whispering, and went on to bemoan the fact that there wasn't a civilized beauty shop within fifty miles.

Glorianna glanced up from the coat of vermillion polish she was applying to the squat nails of Mrs. Tucker, the plumber's wife. Glorianna only got red, but Mrs. Tucker got furious, and clucked like a rooster. Claudia stepped on Nancy's foot, and made discreet signs. Nancy didn't know what it was all about. She fumbled with the switch of the motor until she finally managed to turn it off. "What's the matter?" she boomed out into the silence. She seemed a little startled at her own volume, and began over again. "What did you want to tell me?" she asked with careful modulation.

"I wanted to tell you not to talk so loud!" Claudia shouted.

"Ssh—don't yell," Nancy reproved her. "Come over for bridge tonight—oh, I always forget, you don't play bridge, but come over anyway, I'm having a crowd up from town for the weekend."

"I don't think we can," Claudia evaded. "David has some work to do." (It was all he needed, to go over to Nancy's, who gave him a pain.)

Nancy compressed the youthless cupid's bow of her scarlet lips. "You tell David for me," said she, "that he's a fool. He ought to take a vacation. I saw him this morning at the station. He looks terrible."

Claudia could feel her bones turn to water, for

Nancy's words lent reality to her fear. Suppose David didn't find his way out of the woods? The world was full of men who hadn't found their way. George Riddle had been one of them, so Nancy knew what she was talking about. "He drinks," people had always said of him. And then during the depression, he was found with a bullet through his head. It was one of the reasons why Nancy acted silly and dyed her hair, and tried to forget that he had done it so that she might have his life insurance.

"I'm ready for you, Mrs. Naughton," Glorianna called across the room.

A manicure seemed grotesquely unimportant now. Claudia sank into the chair, left warm from the solid rear of the plumber's wife, and regretted that she had not let it cool off. If there was one thing she couldn't abide it was a warmed-up seat.

Glorianna rustled herself into position on the other side of the table, and lifted Claudia's hand for a brief inspection. "My, my, my," she said.

"My, my, my, is right," Claudia agreed.

"Never mind, we'll fix these naughty nails so you won't recognize them," Glorianna promised with an acquired optimism. "Isn't it a simply peachy day?"

"Peachy," Claudia assented.

"It's certainly been lovely weather we're having," Glorianna continued. She picked up the file. "Would you like your nails shorter?"

"No. Longer, please."

"Okie doke," Glorianna chirped, before she blinked.

That'll learn her, reflected Claudia brutally. She reached for a near-by pile of magazines. It was virtually the same pile she had gone through last season, thumbed and dirty, and mostly about hygiene. She picked one up anyway, and held it in front of her as a barrier to further conversation.

Glorianna thought she really wanted to read. "That's one of the old magazines," she said. "I just keep them around to look nice. I've got the new *Astrology*, though, if you'd like to see it." She opened a drawer in the table, and withdrew from a jumble of hairpins and curlers a crisp pamphlet bound in silver-colored paper. "Go on, look through it. There's a general forecast for Gemini in this issue. What's your sign?"

"Sign?"

"I mean are you Libra or Taurus or Sagittarius or what?"

"I don't think I'm anything," said Claudia.

Glorianna emitted a squeal of amusement. "Everybody is, you have to be, or you wouldn't be born! I mean you'd be born maybe, but the minute you are, you've got a sign."

"Nobody ever told me about it," said Claudia, suppressing a yawn.

"Don't you know anything about astrology?" Glorianna demanded in amazement.

"I'm afraid not much."

"For mercy sakes," said Glorianna. "What month is your birthday?"

"December."

"Beginning or end?"

"End."

"You're Capricorn," Glorianna announced. "The sign of the goat. Soak please." She led Claudia's fingers to a bowl of milky water. "Capricorn people are born to burden and struggle, they have to overcome obstacles," she continued. "Like a goat, I suppose, climbing over rocks."

Claudia frowned. "I don't think I care for that," she said.

"A lot of writers and artists are Capricorn," Glorianna pointed out.

"That's nice," said Claudia, slightly mollified.

"Personally," Glorianna went on, "I'd rather be my own sign. The beginning of this year is terrible for Gemini people, but it's going to end up beautifully provided we fight with the current and not against it. Uranus and Saturn are going to remain until May 1942, but anyway we're standing on the threshold of achievement."

It was Claudia's turn to blink. Glorianna had become an intellectual giant, disguised by a permanent wave and a small high giggle. "Where'd you learn all that?" she asked humbly.

"From the astrology magazine," said Glorianna.

"I go by it in everything. That's why I did my shop over. It says Gemini has to rise over self-imposed limitations this year."

"Hey there!" Nancy boomed from across the room. "I'm dry, come and take me out!"

Glorianna rose. "Excuse me while I unpin Mrs. Riddle," she said. "You can soak the other hand awhile."

Claudia soaked the other hand, and with the aid of her elbow shuffled the pages of the astrology magazine until she found the chapter on Gemini. She was more than ever intrigued when she discovered that David, born June twelfth, was also Gemini, and shared the Sign of the Twins with Glorianna. Wait'll I tell him, she thought. He'll be thrilled.

"Say, Claudia!" Nancy ducked like a turtle, from the electric cylinder, and gathered her lap together. "I'll give you the name of a wonderful woman, if you want. I just went to her."

Nancy was an eternal reservoir of "wonderful" names, from chiropractors to upholsterers. Claudia enquired, a little wearily, "A wonderful woman for what?"

"Horoscopes," said Nancy. "She did mine. She charges a hundred dollars, but it's worth it. She gave me a full future, and told me everything that ever happened in the past."

"I'll use my memory," said Claudia. "It's cheaper." Her heart beat a little faster. "And I don't want to know what the future holds. I'm satisfied with the present."

"Same here," said Glorianna. "Anyway, this magazine answers the same purpose for a quarter. It's a daily guide, besides. I look at it every morning before I go to work."

"What'd it say about today?" asked Claudia, feeling that she was getting something for nothing, for David.

"It said," Glorianna recited glibly, " '*Curb irritability. Avoid depression. Evening favorable to romance and pleasure.*' "

"Always grateful for small favors," Claudia murmured. She turned back to the magazine, and found the chapter on Capricorn. "Let's see what it says about me, for today." How nice if her evening, too, were to bring romance and pleasure. It was high time for David to act human for a change.

"*Cooperate with business associates—*" No, that was yesterday. And she'd certainly done it too, what with breaking her back and her nails on transplanting cabbages.

"What's it tell you?" Glorianna asked with interest.

"Friday," Claudia read aloud. "*Avoid accidents. Keep out of cars. Guard against deception. Wait for developments.*"

"I wouldn't worry about the accident part of it," Glorianna reassured her. "It doesn't mean anything."

"Doesn't it?" Claudia asked in an odd voice. Glorianna evidently didn't know that if she, Claudia, had got hold of this twenty-five cent document in time, she'd have saved the price of a garage door. And as for the reference to avoiding deception—if it wasn't deception to deceive a butcher into donating dog bones for family use, then she didn't know the meaning of the word. The whole thing of course might be coincidence, but if it was, it had an extremely long arm.

Fascinated, she ran her finger up the page to see what her horoscope had to say about last Sunday. It would be funny, if again it hit the nail upon the head. But unfortunately, just as she found the place, Glorianna started to buff her nails, and she didn't have any hands left to hold the book with.

"Where do I get one of these little magazines?" she asked, clearing her throat nonchalantly.

"Any newsstand," said Glorianna.

Claudia went on clearing her throat. "Not that I believe in it," she added, with a little laugh.

"But it's scientific!" Glorianna protested.

"Even Hitler," said Nancy, becoming Glorianna's ally, "wouldn't make a move without consulting his astrologist."

Glorianna nodded. "Everyone knows that," she said.

"I didn't," said Claudia meekly. "What about Roosevelt?"

"I couldn't say about Roosevelt," Glorianna reluctantly admitted. "But I wouldn't be surprised."

Of course the first thing Jane asked was, "Where's the bacon and the bones?"

"I didn't stop for them," said Claudia. "I was in a hurry to get home."

She sped to her room. In a few minutes Jane followed. She looked surprised when she saw Claudia reading. "I thought maybe something was wrong the way you rushed upstairs," she said.

Claudia dropped the magazine out of Jane's line of vision. "Is there anything you want?" she asked patiently.

"Yes, Matthew cut his finger. But it was a clean cut, and I bandaged it up. Do you want to see it?"

"Later," said Claudia.

"Your sister-in-law telephoned—nothing important."

"Then tell me afterwards," Claudia entreated.

At that point Jane seemed to gather that her presence was unwelcome. She started to leave and then remembered her original mission. "Lunch is on the table," she mentioned diffidently.

There was even less privacy after lunch. Edward had to take Majesty to the bull, and while he was gone the sheep scrambled through the fence on to the road, and it was a job to chase them back where they belonged. Then the vacuum man came about the vacuum, and after that Jane needed some moral support on the matter of disposing of a batch of Matthew's outgrown rompers. It was after four o'clock before Claudia finally managed to escape to her room. She closed the door, and took the magazine out of her bureau drawer. A knock sounded. She thrust the book behind her and called, "Come in," trying to sound pleasant about it, because she knew that it was Jane again.

Jane said, "I hate to disturb you, Mrs. Naughton, but you didn't bring the bacon for supper, and kidneys don't taste like anything without bacon."

"On the contrary, they taste more like kidneys," said Claudia. "But I'll remember to bring some on my way to the station to call for Mr. Naughton. . . . And for Heaven's sake," she added to herself, "get out and let me read in peace."

The end of it was that she locked herself in the bathroom to avoid a conversation with the lightning-rod man, who had to go up to the attic to get out on the roof. He always wanted to talk about lightning rods for the barn, and wouldn't it be a great deal less expensive than having a fire? I'm in no mood to talk about problematical fires that never happen, she thought grimly, and thrust the bolt across the door.

In a little while she heard Bobby on the stairs. She heard him go from one room to another. There wasn't any urgency in his footsteps, he merely wanted to find her. Well, he wasn't going to find her, she exulted, and remained perversely silent, waiting for him to go out to the garden to look for her. But a kind of sixth sense led him to the bathroom. He banged on the door. "Mother!"

She closed her eyes and compressed her lips.

"Mother!" He banged again.

"What is it!" she cried hoarsely.

"Are you in there?"

"Where do you think I am? Run outside in the air."

"I was in the air already."

"Not enough. Go on and play."

"I did play. Mother, I have to talk to you!"

"What about?"

It was obvious that there was little, if anything on his mind. It was merely the magnetlike attraction that she seemed to possess for everyone in the house. "Look," she announced with stark finality, "I'm not talking."

"Why?" he asked simply.

"Because I'm busy."

"What are you doing?"

Her voice grated. "What do you think I'm doing! I'm sitting on the edge of the bathtub reading a book!"

"Oh," said Bobby.

When she came out humming, an hour later, Jane was straightening the linen closet in the upper hall.

Jane looked puzzled, and Claudia didn't blame her. She thought, If Bobby ever acted as funny as I've been acting all afternoon, I'd make it my business to investigate.

Her heart was light as she drove to the station. It was weeks since she had felt so carefree. With the frugal expenditure of twenty-five cents, she had bought complete freedom from worry and responsibility. It was in the nature of a revelation to realize that everything she did, and everything she didn't do was directed by the planets. Take this morning for example. There was no need to berate herself for smashing the garage door—she had simply been a tool in the hands of Jupiter. The difficulty, of course, would lie in getting David to accept that fact, for she had an uncomfortable foreboding that the very word astrology would act as a red flag to his masculinity, particularly if he knew that she had come by the revelation in Glorianna's Beauty Shoppe. It was going to be even more difficult to make him realize that his own troubles were sidereal rather than personal. Whatever he was going through was a kind of test that the heavens had set for him, and, according to his Gemini forecast, he would emerge a finer, better person from these months of trial and conflict. But I'll have to be awfully tactful the way I tell it to him, she reflected dubiously.

She pulled up in the station square just as the train was coming in. She tooted the horn and he waved to her from the steps. In spite of her newly formed assurance, her spirits fell. Stars or no stars, he looked tired and discouraged, and his step lacked the spring with which he used to hurry toward her.

They kissed out of the window. She started to move over to her seat. "Don't bother to move, you can drive," he said, and got in the other side.

Apprehension tightened its hold on her. He was really sick if he let her drive. She stepped on the starter and released the clutch, devoutly hoping that all the accidents in her horoscope were over for that day. Now, if ever, was the time to put her best foot forward. She must give him no loophole of criticism, she must be cautious, smooth and considerate of her motor. Unfortunately she was so very considerate that she stalled once or twice. "Don't let it die, get a move on, you're not going to a funeral!" he adjured her sharply.

It was all she could do not to throw the car in his face. But she remembered that he was not to blame. Silently, she recited his daily horoscope like a lesson. "*Curb irritability. Avoid depression. Evening brings romance and pleasure.*" She said, penitently, "I'm sorry I stalled, dear. I'll try not to do it again."

He eyed her in distrust. She thought, That was a tactical error, I should have argued. She sought to cover her indiscretion. "I had an awfully interesting day," she continued brightly.

"Doing what?"

"Oh, lots of things." She gave a light little laugh. "By the way, did you know your sign was the Twins?"

"One of me is plenty," he said sourly. "What are you talking about?"

"Well, it's a long story."

"Make it short, please."

She swallowed her misgivings. "To begin with, I had a manicure. I took the dogs. They loved it. And I met Nancy Riddle—"

"That idiot woman," he broke in. "That pink-haired jackass on two feet."

"Aren't you ashamed to be so intolerant!"

"No, I'm not ashamed!" he stuck up for himself. "Why should I be ashamed!"

"Don't lose your temper. She means well."

"God save me from people who mean well."

"She's really fond of us though. She asked us over tonight; she's having people up from New York."

He emitted a grunt of antagonism. "Oh, I said we wouldn't go," Claudia hastened to soothe him. She tried a completely fresh attack. "Elizabeth's house is coming along very well, I think."

This time he gave a growl instead of a grunt. "It's costing twice what we'd figured with these damn labor conditions. Masons want fifteen dollars a day. . . . Step on it, Claudia, what's the idea of crawling along?"

"You always said I shouldn't go more than forty!"

"You were going thirty."

"I wasn't. The speedometer looks different from where you're sitting. . . . Did you have a hard day, dear?" she digressed with dogged amiability.

"Pretty. The news is rotten tonight. We're asleep on our feet."

She glanced at him. Bitterness and disillusion stared out of his tired eyes. Fear rose in her anew. His weakened spirit was fertile soil for the horror of the world. Part of the trouble with him was that he couldn't tune out of what was going on. It's not our war, she thought rebelliously. He has no right to let it get him like that.

Aloud she said, determined to pull him back to his own small universe, "Matthew cut his finger today."

"On what?"

"He fished one of your razor blades out of the scrap basket. After you'd wrapped it all up, too."

"Serves him right," said David.

"Both your sons are going to grow up to be garbage collectors. Bobby's just as bad."

"Careful of this truck," said David. "Pull over."

"I saw it. I am. . . . Edward took Majesty this afternoon."

He came to life at that. "Did he? How was it, do you know?"

"I didn't ask him. Isn't it always the same?"

"Not always."

"Why not?"

"Cows are as temperamental as women."

"What about bulls?"

"Here, I'll drive," he said. "Draw up and move over."

He feels better, Claudia concluded as she relinquished her place to him. "I hope you realize I was driving faultlessly," she reminded him, building up to the garage door. The thing to do was to keep him from seeing it until she had had a chance to explain about the stars. She wanted to use the accident as an asset instead of a liability.

They crossed the bridge and came in sight of the house. "I'll take the car around to the garage, and you go on up and relax before dinner," she suggested.

"No, I'll put it away—I want to see Edward."

Courage deserted her. There was no law that she had to be at his side when he discovered the damage. "Then I'll get out at the front gate. Jane's waiting for the bacon," she said. "But I wish you'd kiss me first," she added wistfully.

Absently he dropped a light peck against her cheek. "That was no kiss," she grumbled.

Obligingly, he delivered one of his unerring whacks across the backside. That'll be the last friendly gesture he'll make for some time, she thought with a sigh.

Jane received the bacon in grateful surprise. She had evidently given up all hope of getting it. "Supper's ready whenever you are," she said.

"Better wait a little while," said Claudia nervously. She wanted all the fireworks to be over before the meal began.

She was in her closet, pretending to look for a sweater when David entered the bedroom a short while later.

"Nice job you did with the garage door," he remarked at once.

She stuck her head out. "What?"

"You heard me."

"Oh. The garage door."

"Yes. The garage door."

She smiled quizzically. "I suppose you think I did it?"

"I don't think. I know. I recognized your fine handiwork in every splinter of it."

His high and mighty manner destroyed her control. "Kindly reserve your judgment. You don't know the first thing about it!"

"Did you or did you not crash into it?"

She refused to be cornered. "In a manner of speaking, yes; in a manner of speaking, no."

"I'm in no mood for riddles."

"This isn't a riddle." She took a deep breath, and came brazenly out with it. "Did you ever hear of astrology?"

He looked at her. "My God," he said merely.

"Don't 'my God' me!" she flared, throwing tact

and discretion to the winds. "It wasn't my fault! And if you don't believe me, read this!"

She picked up the magazine from the table, already opened to the page whereon her daily horoscope was heavily underscored in pencil, and thrust it at him. He took it from her slowly, and read it aloud, giving each word its measured due. "*Avoid accidents. Keep out of cars. Wait for developments.*" His voice came to an end, and he just stood there staring at her.

"Say something!" she rasped.

"You don't actually believe this nonsense?"

"Oh, I suppose you're too masculine to believe in astrology?"

"A hell of a long sight too masculine."

"Hitler believes in it!" she flung at him. "He uses his stars to help him at every step!"

"Sure," David readily conceded. "Why not?"

It was a long moment before she saw what he meant. Then she said flatly, "It's not possible."

"Well, look at Bluff and Bluster," David replied. "And anyway, since when are you and Hitler chums?"

"Don't be silly," she said. "All right, don't take Hitler for an example. There are dozens of virile bankers and lawyers who swear by their horoscopes. Just wait till you read your own before you scoff."

"I'll wait a long time, my child." He put the book gently upon the table. "A very long time indeed."

She could have wept with frustration and rage. She had known it would be this way. "You and your mind!" she sputtered. "Your wonderful masculine strong-minded mind! I could wring its neck!"

"Listen," he broke in, wearily. "I'm dog tired, and your gabbling annoys me."

"Gabbling," she muttered.

"Yes, gabbling," he said.

It was one of their less pleasant suppers. He scolded Bobby for not finishing his plate, and then filled the child with a sense of deep injustice by eating next to nothing himself. "I'm going up for my pipe," he said, after he had drunk two cups of black coffee.

"Bobby'll get it for you," Claudia offered, heaping coals of fire on his head.

"No, thanks. He couldn't find the one I want."

Jane came in to clear the table. "Such nice kidneys," she mourned. "Mr. Naughton will run himself down."

"I know he will," said Claudia desperately. "I'm worried to death about him."

Jane shook her head. "It doesn't pay to worry," she said. "Everything comes out like it should be, in the end."

Claudia threw a quick glance at her. For a brief instant, she thought she detected a glint of horoscope in Jane's serene dark eyes, but she couldn't be sure. Believing in the stars was probably something that wise people kept unto themselves. "Just the same," she decided, "I'll have the book down here in case I can get him to let me read a couple of things aloud to him."

She ran upstairs for it. She looked on the table. She was certain she had left it there, but it was gone. Could Bobby have taken it? She walked into the nursery, where he was getting into bed by slow degrees. "You didn't see a book, did you, dear?"

"What kind of a book?"

"A little magazine, about so big."

He looked intelligent. "The one you were reading in the bathroom this afternoon?"

"Yes. Where is it?"

"I saw Daddy take it in the bathroom a little while ago. I guess he's reading it in there too."

"Oh," said Claudia.

For the second time in the past weeks, wisdom visited at her shoulder. She went down to the living room and sat on the sofa, and looked at the advertisements in the evening paper. Minutes passed. Finally she heard the latch on the bathroom door click, and open. David's step, quick and alive, sounded on the boards above her head. He was going back to the bedroom. He was whistling. He hadn't whistled for ages.

He came down eventually, packing his pipe with tobacco. He stood behind her and nuzzled his nose into the back of her neck, in his old way. "Hello," he said.

"Hello," she answered.

"Look," he said. "Do you want to go over to that idiot's party? If you do, I'll take you."

She couldn't believe her ears. "You mean you'd go with me to Nancy's?"

"I'm a lout," he said. "You've been sticking in the house entirely too much."

"But I like sticking in the house," she said. "And you're not a lout."

He bent and kissed her again. It was getting to be a real kiss, with romance and pleasure creeping into it. His horoscope was working, but he didn't know it. "I love you, you little fool," he muttered, out of the clear blue.

A hundred birds started to sing inside of her, for there was a look about him that made her know that he was emerging from dark woods into sunlight and air. Never mind what had led him there, never mind whence the lift had come, it was enough that it had happened.

He sat down on the sofa beside her and pulled her over to his lap. "Claudia, listen to me. You don't really believe in that astrological nonsense, do you? Nine-tenths of it is pure coincidence."

She quelled the impulse to question him about the other tenth. "Of course I don't believe in it," she assured him guilelessly.

He seemed relieved. "Would you like to take a ride or anything?"

"I don't think so."

"Walk?"

"I'd really rather stay home, if you don't mind."

"I don't mind." He kissed her long and hard this time, as if he'd just got back from a long journey. She closed her eyes, and gave a secret smile. Her own horoscope was working, too. She would not have to do another thing, except sit very still, and await developments.

Three

ONE MINUTE IT WAS LABOR DAY, HOT AND STICKY, AND
the next minute it was almost Thanksgiving, with
winter and the flu just around the corner. Even Dr.
Barry in the village was down with it, and Bobby
reported with a degree of pride that there were only
seven children left in his class at school. "They're
all home sick," said he, and Claudia sent up a swift,
silent prayer of gratitude that so far there wasn't so
much as a sniffle in the Naughton household. It was
almost too good to be true, what with Matthew cut-
ting his second-year molars, and Bobby at the age
when his nose either ran or got stopped up at the
slightest provocation.

Julia, who happened to hear him one rainy day
when she stopped in on her way to Boston, said that
it was probably sinus, poor child. But David said,
nonsense, it was only puberty. Personally, Claudia
thought that Bobby was much too young for puberty, and anyway, she couldn't see how growing
up could be tied to a running nose. However, she
kept a discreet silence on the subject, because she
knew from Julia's experience, that sinus could snow-

ball into a lot of money, and in the end you were apt to be a little worse off than you were when you started. Puberty was certainly a prudent alternative, for now was no time to begin with doctors. It was bad enough to have begun with veterinaries. Every other week or so, it seemed that the cows needed a test for this or that, and the pigs needed an injection against something else.

"This is getting to be expensive," Claudia disapproved. "It would be cheaper to buy our milk and bacon."

"It isn't," David tried to make her understand, "a question of milk and bacon. It's a question of capital investment."

"But is a farm a wise capital investment?" she persisted.

"Find me a better one," said he. "Especially when it's small, productive and diversified."

"We've had to take on day labor even though we are small," she mentioned.

"That again is part of our investment," he explained. "The men we're hiring now aren't taking care of the stock, they're helping build fence, and clear brush."

"I see," said Claudia. Actually, she didn't see anything at all except that he was rationalizing, for investment or not, he was crazy about the farm, and no sacrifice was too much for him to make for it. Even when it came to buying a new suit, he preferred to go without the suit and top-dress the alfalfa field with a ton of fertilizer. However, Claudia kept a discreet silence on that score too, because common sense told her that she was lucky he was in love with the land instead of another woman.

Sometimes she marveled at all these discreet silences she was learning to keep. Was it possible that she was becoming one of those clever, devious wives who handled their husbands with kid gloves? There was no doubt that David was in a kid-glove period, but at the same time it was a kind of spiritual prostitution to subdue her natural reactions in order to maintain a superficial peace. "When things get a little more straightened out with him," she promised herself, "I'm going to let go and say anything I feel like." In the meantime, she smiled and bided her time, though she simply boiled when it came to paying the veterinary ten dollars to visit a sheep on the very same day that Dr. Barry charged only three dollars to visit Matthew's hand. At that, David had the nerve to say it was a lot of hysterical nonsense to get excited about a couple of smashed fingers, though he didn't say boo about the sheep. At which point Claudia spoke her mind freely and fully. "And I say it's a lot of hysterical nonsense," she came back at him, "to get excited because a sheep coughs!"

"Sheep have no fight in them," David defended. "She'd have gone into pneumonia, and she happens to be one of our best ewes."

"Matthew happens to be one of our best children," she retorted. "Suppose I didn't have the doctor and he developed tetanus?"

David pooh-poohed the idea of tetanus, but Claudia said she knew somebody who knew somebody who had neglected a simple little scratch—and died of it.

"Rot," said David—only he didn't say "rot"—"a little knowledge is your complete undoing."

In all fairness, she knew that he was right. Let anyone in the family so much as bat an eyelash, and her imagination would run riot to the most dire complications. She didn't even trust a common cold, and the epidemic of influenza, which was mounting daily, filled her with increasing alarm. It was like waiting for the hand of fate to fall.

It was a relief when it finally happened, with herself as victim. She awakened, one dim and frosty Sunday morning, impressed with a sharp awareness of her physical being. A wave of gratitude interlaced with nausea swept over her. Immediately, she drove a shrewd bargain with the Lord. "God, really I don't mind how sick I am, if You'll let me have all the germs for the whole family—including Jane and Edward," she threw in cannily. If she was going to be laid up, someone had to run the house.

"What time is it?" asked David sleepily.

"Early."

"Then go back to sleep."

It was funny how each one always knew when the

other one was awake. It was doubtless a sign of very great love, but there were times, such as now, when it was inconvenient. She would have enjoyed the luxury of a little moaning and groaning, but that sort of privacy did not exist between them.

She lay very quiet, and eventually drifted off into a restless doze. A crash from the nursery made them both sit up with a start. She was halfway down the hall before David caught up with her. "You'd be a fine one in a war," he upbraided her.

This was manifestly unjust, for he knew perfectly well that she'd be wonderful in a war, as she didn't have an ounce of personal fear. Yet when she reached the nursery, her knees went weak with panic. Matthew lay screaming on the floor, with an upturned chair upon his belly, and his face a mass of blood. Bobby was frightened too. "I didn't push him," he offered unconvincingly. "He climbed out of his crib, and the chair fell over on him. Is he dead?"

"People don't scream when they're dead," said Jane, who had rushed up from the kitchen. "He's only cut his lip."

"Serves him right," said David heartlessly.

Claudia felt that neither he nor Jane was sufficiently concerned. "He fell on the back of his head, how can we be sure it's not a concussion?" she demanded.

"Because it's not," said David.

"You wouldn't be so sure if it were your pig!" she accused him.

"My pig doesn't climb out of bed when he has no business to."

He was being childish, and she started to tell him so, but the floor suddenly turned soft beneath her feet. She caught at the railing of the crib and then scurried back to bed as fast as she could.

To her dismay, she found that Jane, in a burst of efficiency, had already stopped on her way downstairs to strip off the sheets for the next day's laundry.

"Oh, dear," said Claudia, gazing disconsolately at the bare mattress.

"Oh, dear what?" queried David at her shoulder.

"I wanted to go back to bed," she said with a complete and simple honesty.

He misunderstood entirely, and said he had to fix fence with Edward. "See you tonight," he promised jauntily, and jumped into his clothes.

"I'm going with you," Bobby announced from the doorway.

"Yes, take him along," said Claudia. She could hardly wait for the house to settle down to peace and quiet so that she could rest her aching head on the living-room sofa.

They came back at noon, cleaning the mud off their feet on the terrace with a great deal of unnecessary stamping and scraping. Claudia struggled to her feet and pretended to be freshening the fire when they entered. "Here, I'll do that," said David at once. He had a smug illusion that only a man knew how to do things with a fire. "Why didn't you come out-doors this morning?" he said amiably.

"I didn't feel like it. . . . Run and change into dry shoes, Bobby."

"Mad?" David asked when they were alone.

"Why should I be mad?" she returned with her mind on her stomach.

Still he felt that something was wrong, although he couldn't quite put his finger on it. "Is Matthew all right? Do you want me to look at him?" he suggested magnanimously.

"No don't, please. He's taking his nap."

He studied her closed face. "Listen," he protested wryly, "I didn't do anything. Honest."

It was funny to see him so conciliatory over nothing. She debated whether it would be kinder to spoil his Sunday by telling him that she felt sick enough to die, or just let him go on thinking that she was nursing a grievance. She compromised by saying, "Don't be silly."

Fortunately—or unfortunately—they were having one of their own ducks for dinner, and he attributed her lack of appetite to a purely sentimental reaction. "Don't be so female," he said. "It's no different from buying at a store. Here, just taste this," he insisted. "It's delicious."

He held forth a piece of breast, which she sampled gingerly. She was in no mood to mince words. "It's tough," she said.

David scowled. "You're crazy." He took a second helping, doubtlessly deluding himself with the conviction that his capital investment was at long last paying dividends. "Next Sunday, we'll have a suckling pig," he announced.

She shuddered violently.

"I noticed you ate chicken last week," he reminded her.

"The chicken was too worn out to care any more."

He was quick to take offense. "Firstly that's not true. And secondly, if you think we're going to kill off any birds that are young enough to lay, you've got another think coming."

"Oh, now I see how it's going to work," she rejoined ironically. "We're never going to be able to eat anything that isn't ossified with old age."

It was an unwise comment, for it brought them right back to the suckling pig. "I think if you don't mind," she excused herself, with haste, "I'll go upstairs."

"A fine farmer's wife you turned out to be!" he called after her.

She wanted to retort that her original marriage contract had not mentioned the compulsory consumption of ancient livestock, but the zest for repartee abruptly deserted her. She made for the bedroom as fast as she could, only to find that Shakespeare had already taken possession of the chaise longue.

"Be so kind," she requested coldly.

He made no move, apparently under the impression that a complete suspension of his faculties rendered him invisible to the human eye. She yanked him up, but he merely dangled, long and boneless in her grasp, his eyes averted, and his ears laid flat. "Oh, Shakespeare darling," she suddenly whimpered, burying her face in his soft fur, "I feel so sick."

The unexpected endearment brought him to life. His ears tipped forward, and his amber eyes widened. He began to purr, loudly and without tact. "You should worry," said Claudia bitterly. "Scat!"

He took his own good time about it, carrying his tail in an impudent salute, and flaunting the white bloomers on his hind legs. Out in the hall, he collided with Bobby. Bobby was full of a rich and fraudulent emotion. "Hello, my lovely beautiful Shakespeare!" he effused. "Do you know where my mother is?"

Shakespeare evidently saw no reason why he should talk. "All right for you," said Bobby. He raised his voice shrilly. "Mother! Where are you!"

Ignominiously she adopted Shakespeare's technique. She closed her eyes and kept very still, and discovered that it worked. Bobby rushed off downstairs in search of her, but she knew that in a few minutes he would be back again on her trail. She sighed, and dragged herself to the medicine chest in the bathroom. She couldn't find a single thing to make her feel better, however, for neither she nor

David were pill-takers. Only the top shelf bore testimony of past skirmishes with croup and earache and poison ivy, and she regarded with disfavor the heterogeneous array of old prescriptions that had long since outlived their function. Saving empty bottles against a rainy day, she abruptly decided, was a thankless form of thrift that seldom, if ever, bore fruit. She had no doubt that if an emergency ever did arise, she could always find an empty bottle somewhere. Now's the time to get rid of this collection, she told herself. After all, there was nothing in her compact with the Lord to rule out a lengthy illness or a quick demise, and in either event she didn't want to leave an untidy medicine chest chalked up against her.

Judging by the way she felt, there wasn't a moment to lose. She set to work at once. Bobby drifted to the threshold as she cleared the shelves of their final bit of clutter. "I was looking all over for you," he said reproachfully.

"Well now that you've found me, what do you want?"

"Nothing," he admitted. He caught sight of the well-filled wastebasket beside her. His hand reached down. Automatically, she slapped it away. "Not a chance," said she.

"But I have to have that bottle with the gold top," he besought her.

"It's not gold, and even if it were, you wouldn't want it."

"But I do! I can make something out of it."

"What?"

"I don't know yet. But I can."

"Listen," she told him. "You're just a little junk collector from away back. Now run along."

He looked so wistful that her heart melted. "Here," she said, "give me your palm."

She picked up the gold-topped bottle and shook a few remaining drops of lotion into his outstretched paw. "Rub it in," she said. "It'll make your hands nice and soft."

He was both horrified and affronted as the thick fragrant liquid touched his skin. "I don't like it!" he protested, for all the world like David. "I smell like a girl!"

"Well, supposing? Better men than you have smelled pretty."

"I'm not going to stay here," he said stiffly.

She shrugged. "You can't hurt my feelings."

David put in an appearance a few moments later. "Hey, don't throw that away!" he expostulated, fishing an old toothbrush out of the basket. "I need it for shoe polish."

"You're your son's own father," she said severely. "Here, let me have your palm." She held the gold-topped bottle poised over his hand, but he was too quick for her. His grip tightened like a vise around her wrist. "Drop it," he ordered.

She dropped it.

"What's the idea of cleaning house on a beautiful Sunday afternoon?" he continued. He drew her to the window and scrutinized her closely, since he knew that only advancing crises aroused in her these sporadic attacks of orderliness. "You look like a piece of cheese. Don't you feel well?"

"If you must know," she blurted out, "I've got the flu. I woke up with it this morning."

Without further comment he lifted her in his arms and plumped her down on the bed. "Not on the good spread!" she cried.

"Never mind the good spread. Where does it hurt you?"

"No place, and every place."

His fingers encircled her wrist. He knew exactly how to take a pulse, and his touch gave forth a curious strength and healing. "You should have been a doctor," she told him, which was another way of saying that she loved him.

"Damn shame I wasn't," he agreed. "Open."

"Open what?"

"Your mouth, what do you think?"

"My throat doesn't hurt, and my tongue is fine."

"Do you want to open it by yourself?" he asked her pleasantly, "or would you like me to open it for you?"

She said, "I hate you."

He twisted her head, this way and that, to catch the light. "You haven't got the flu," he affirmed. "You're just hungry."

"I'm not!" she denied indignantly.

He paid no attention to her. "You didn't eat enough lunch. I'll ask Jane to fix you something."

"You'll do nothing of the sort. Jane's getting Matthew up."

"Then I'll fix it myself."

She snorted. There were some men who could cook, and some who couldn't. David couldn't, and it was another of the things she loved about him.

"Let's see," he went on. "How about some hot tea?"

Hot tea. She pondered on it, a little longingly. She wasn't the sort of person who drank tea as a rule, but a lot of people swore by it, and perhaps it would take away that sinking feeling in the pit of her stomach. "You wouldn't know how to make it," she challenged him maliciously.

"Oh, I wouldn't?" He placed an extra log on the fire and poked up a bright blaze. "Stay there, and don't budge. I'll be back in a minute."

She lay against the pillows and closed her eyes, and thought how wonderful it was to have a husband and an open fireplace in your bedroom that actually burned. She felt a yearning compassion for the vast multitude of women who were alone and lonely. She thought of Elizabeth and Nancy, and her heart ached for them. Elizabeth was probably reading, and Nancy was probably playing bridge. No one person has a right to have as much as I have, she thought humbly. The sound of her household was like a hymn —Matthew's wakening chatter, the blare of Bobby's favorite radio program, the banging of cupboard doors as David moved about the kitchen below.

He returned after a considerable time, bearing a tray laid with a dish towel. The cup and saucer on the tray didn't match, and the tea looked black as ink. "I made you a sandwich, too," he said, apropos of a high, lopsided edifice that reposed in the center of one of her best dinner plates.

"What on earth have you got in it?" she exclaimed, for, besides being mammouth, it leaked indecently at every point.

He counted off on his fingers. "Ham, cheese, lettuce, sliced radish, mustard, mayonnaise, and a slice of duck."

"It's obscene."

"Well, don't eat it," he said, and tactfully busied himself with the fire.

A silence fell upon the room. "I wouldn't want to disappoint you," she murmured, "after you went to so much trouble."

Despite its vulgar redundancy, it was the best sandwich she had ever put her teeth in. Even the crusts were tasty.

"I feel wonderful," she confessed. She was ashamed of herself—it was rather like backing out of her bargain with the Lord—but there it was. "I really ought to get up and finish the medicine chest. Although if you're quite sure I'm not going to die, why should I bother?"

"Only the good die young," said David. "Would you like some company?"

She was cagey. "What kind of company?"

For answer, he lay down beside her, first emptying his pipe like a gentleman. "I don't mind your smoking," she said generously.

"I'll smoke later." He slipped his arm beneath her head.

"You've got a lot of muscle," she said.

"Don't you like it?"

"It feels like I'm lying on a rock. But I like it fine."

A car drove up and stopped. The dogs began to bark. David cursed softly and sweetly, as befitted his mood. "Don't look a gift car in the face," Claudia reproved him. "Maybe it's a man to buy another pig."

"No such luck," said David. Last Sunday had been a red-letter day. A farmer had seen their advertisement in a local paper the year before, and had finally gotten around to answering it. Fortunately, Ruby had a brand new litter, and he'd bought one.

"I'll get up and see," said Claudia, overcome with curiosity. She hurried to the window. "It certainly looks like someone for pigs," she reported. "It's an old car, square in the backside and high up in the air."

"It's the ad," said David with satisfaction. "Guaranteed to work in twelve months."

"How much do we make when we sell a pig for three dollars and seventy-five cents?" she asked.

"Actually," he replied with honesty, "we lose a little. Theoretically we make about twenty per cent on our original investment."

"Which is better—to be actual or theoretical?"

His eyes narrowed. "Are you being dumb, or just nasty?"

"Neither," she assured him innocently. "I just wanted to know."

"I don't think you really love the farm," he said.

"Darling, I adore it." She stood looking down at him. He was rugged and handsome in his rough clothes, with all the tired lines gone out of his face, and the tension of the week wiped clear. "I adore the farm," she repeated, "because of what it means to you."

"That's not enough."

"All right then, I adore it without qualification. In fact," she added, "I think it's a wonderful capital investment in these times."

He seemed a little puzzled. "You're a funny one," he said.

"Don't you love me?"

"I adore you." He caught her to him. "And I mean *adore* you," he repeated huskily.

It was a moment that they needed together—to cement their marriage, or leave a little rift that they would scarcely know was there, and, not knowing, would never try to bridge.

"Ought we go down to see if it's really someone to buy something?" Claudia whispered.

"The hell with somebody to buy something," said David.

Bobby came panting to the threshold. They favored him with an unwelcoming stare. "Now what do you want?" they demanded in unison.

He was too full of news to notice their lack of cordiality. "Guess who's downstairs?" he cried, hopping with excitement.

"We know who's downstairs," said Claudia. "It's a man about a pig."

"Tell him to go out and talk to Edward," said David.

"But it's Fritz and Bertha!" Bobby managed to interpolate. "They drove all the way out from New York to see us! Bertha says her cousin lent him their automobile to do it in!"

"You're a little mixed on pronouns, but I get the general idea," said David sourly.

"I think it's lovely of them," Claudia exclaimed with ostentatious loyalty. "Tell them we'll be right down." She turned to David severely. "And we have to go down—there's no way out of it."

David used a four-letter word and made it sound

like a love song. Claudia pulled his arm. "Anyway, I'm very touched by their faithfulness," she defended. "When your old help keeps coming back to you, it shows you're nice people."

"Or they're nice people," he amended.

They found Bertha sitting on a chair in the kitchen, looking painfully decent in a black coat with a brown fur collar, and a neat velvet hat, heavy with crown. She was dangling Matthew on her knee, trying to rouse in him some vestige of remembrance. But the era of Jane had long since erased from his mind all memory of Bertha's devotion. He permitted himself to be dangled, but his small round face was stony and a little bored. Claudia, pausing in the doorway, sensed a look of real loss in Bertha's china-blue eyes. "You don't remember how Bertha took you to the park in New York?" she was saying, wistfully. "How we used to buy peanuts to feed the squirrels?"

"No," said Matthew with finality. His detached stare remained riveted on an area of Bertha's person halfway between her chin and stomach. "I want to get down," he decided.

Bertha turned the snub into a graceful compliment directed at Jane. "How nice he talks now," she said generously.

Jane, who was washing up the aftermath of David's sandwich making, acknowledged the gesture with an overbalanced politeness. "He talks very nicely for his age," she said. "He's a very bright child altogether," she took pains to assert, lest his failure to make a fuss over Bertha be counted against him.

"Surely he's a very bright child," Bertha agreed heartily. "Bobby's a very bright child, too."

"They're both bright children," said Jane.

Claudia, who had lingered in the doorway, stepped in to relieve this strain of amiability. "Hello, Bertha!"

"Ach, Miss Claudia!"

Claudia laid her cheek for an instant against Bertha's soft face. "It's awfully nice to see you, Bertha! I'm so glad you came. And Bobby was beside himself with joy."

"But Matthew don't remember me," said Bertha sadly.

"The ungrateful little so-and-so," said David, buttoning himself into his lumber jacket. "Hello, Bertha! Grand to see you. Where's Fritz?"

"Bobby took him already to the barn," said Bertha.

"Good," said David. "I'll go out and joint them. See you later."

"Wouldn't you like some coffee or something?" Claudia asked.

"Ach, no, we had dinner on the road. And Jane already asked us."

"'Twould be no trouble at all," Jane reiterated.

"No, no," said Bertha. "Thank you."

Claudia thought, This'll go on forever, like a vicious circle. An idea came to her. "Would you like to see all the improvements we've made in the barn, Bertha?"

Bertha rose with alacrity. "Ach, surely!" On the way to the barn she said, "You have a very good girl, I think. Her kitchen was nice and clean."

"Yes," Claudia nodded, refraining from making too much of Jane's definitely superior qualities. "Do you think the children grew since you saw them at Christmas?"

"I should say so. They grew very tall. And I think Mr. David looks good, too. Very good."

"Oh, I'm glad," said Claudia gratefully. It was as if Bertha had laid a million dollars at her feet.

"But you don't look so very good though," Bertha continued with a frown.

Claudia laughed. "That's all right. If anybody has to look badly, I'd much rather it was me."

"Yah, I'm the same way," said Bertha, with perfect understanding.

It was pleasant to get out of the bleak wind into the warm barn. The three men and Bobby were hanging over the pigpen, absorbed in Ruby's output. "A fine big litter," Fritz was saying. "She's a good sow."

"There's a thrifty individual over there in the corner," Edward pointed out. "He'll take a good boar."

Bobby injected wisely, "I know what a boar is, it's a boy-pig."

Fritz's funny uneven teeth showed out from his

nice smile. "We're going to have a farmer out of
Bobby," he prophesied.

"I hope," said David devoutly.

Claudia crowded among them to look at the young
pigs, mincing around like small, plump women in
short-vamped pumps. Animals were so complete at
birth, she marveled, so utterly perfect in miniature.
Majesty's heifer calf, staring in from an adjoining pen
was only three weeks old, but she was already a mas-
caraed debutante, strong, yet vulnerable in her swift
budding. A barn's a wonderful place, thought Claudia,
a little awed. She smiled at Fritz. "It's nice, isn't it?"
she said simply.

"It's wonderful," said Fritz, from his very depths.
"This is getting to be a rich, productive farm. I remember how it was all rocks when we first came.
Mr. David has worked hard to clear this land. He
deserves credit."

David shared the glory. "You worked like a dog,
too," he said. "And Edward here is as fine a herds-
man as I'd ask for."

"He's lovely with the children too," Claudia put
in—for since Edward was Fritz's son-in-law, it was
quite within the limits of diplomacy to praise him.
I wonder if men aren't better individuals than women
anyway, she suddenly wondered, borrowing the
lingo of the farm. At any rate, when you worked
with animals, you became a little better and more
decent than you really were.

David's voice broke in upon her reverie. "Claudia, you look cold," he said. "You and Bertha better go in the house."

She had not been aware that she was shivering, and that the sick empty feeling was creeping back into her bones. The lights from the house beckoned like an old friend from across the lawn. It was hard to measure her steps to Bertha's unsure progress on the rough stone paths and against the looming menace of trees and shrubs. It seemed an eternity before they reached the terrace. She pushed open the doors into the living room, blind to the invitation of burning logs and softly shaded lamps. "I have to get upstairs, Bertha," she gasped.

Bertha followed her. Claudia found herself in bed with a cold cloth on her temples, and a hot water bag at her feet. "So," said Bertha. "That's better."

"This is idiotic," said Claudia.

"It is not," said Bertha. "It is natural."

"Not for me, it isn't. I'm never sick."

"I don't call this a sickness," said Bertha, smiling.

Claudia stared at her. "It's the flu," she said slowly. "Or isn't it?"

Bertha's lids were heavy with portent, and when she spoke, it was as if her voice were an echo of the past: "I bet you twenty cents," said she.

It was a shock. Yet the more Claudia thought about it, the more possible it seemed. She said nothing to David, however. There was no use worrying him

until she knew whether it was true or not. It occurred to her, with a fleeting sense of desolation, that
this should be a high moment in their love. But the
world had become threatening, and the giving of life
to a new soul bore its obligations and its sacrifices.
David would not find it easy to contemplate the expense of another child. They'd spoken of it once or
twice, and he'd said, "Sorry, darling. We'll have to
wait awhile."

It was difficult not to tell him. She had never kept
anything from him before, and the knowledge
weighed upon her. She spent the evening with her
monthly accounts banked like a shield in front of her
telltale face. Once or twice he looked up from some
blueprints to ask her how she felt, and she said,
"Much better." The piercing sweetness of the afternoon subsided into the unimpassioned union of two
people living prosaically under a single roof. Already,
the land was withdrawing its magic and its healing.
David was girding himself for the day ahead, the
week ahead, the year ahead. His eyes had lost their
peace.

She lay awake for a long while, not moving, so
that he would not know she was awake. Panic assailed her. "Dear God, don't let it be true. Not now."

She could not bear the uncertainty. She thought
of going to see Dr. Barry the first thing in the morning, but if she started out with him, she'd probably
have to keep on with him. David wouldn't like that.

It would mean having the baby in some hospital in Bridgeport. Bridgeport was just a place to pass through as quickly as possible on the way to New York—it was not a place to have anybody say he was born in. "I'd better stick to Dr. Rowland," she concluded. "After all he knows me inside out."

She planned to catch the ten o'clock train to town, which puzzled Jane. She said, "I'd have thought you'd have drove in with Mr. Naughton this morning."

"I didn't want him to know I was going. I have a secret date."

Jane laughed. It was odd, thought Claudia, that sometimes the easiest way to lie was to tell the truth. She wondered that Jane didn't catch on, as Bertha had. Bertha had had a family of her own, perhaps that made the difference. Besides Jane had her hands full this morning with other people's children and had no time to be sentient. Bobby went off to school without eating his cereal, and Matthew was cranky and fretful. "It's those molars," Jane worried.

Claudia felt guilty in leaving her with an upset household, but it wasn't as if she were going off to a sale, or anything of that sort. Moreover she felt pretty miserable herself, and her absence would be less complicating than her presence. "I'll take an early train back," she promised. "And I'll probably bring you all a present," she added.

"You mustn't bother," said Jane.

"There are quite a lot of answers to that," said Claudia.

Edward took her to the station in the truck. Ordinarily she enjoyed riding in the truck. It was high, and jolting and smelled pleasantly of farm. But today she didn't enjoy it at all. She closed her eyes and gritted her teeth.

By the time she reached Dr. Rowland's office she had done a little remembering, and a great deal of figuring. In the end there was no doubt in her mind as to the very day and hour that the baby would arrive —June 14th—practically David's birthday.

Dr. Rowland was equally certain in his diagnosis, but less explicit. "Sometime in June," he confirmed, without enthusiasm. Either he was tired of bringing babies, or he regretted having begun with the junior Naughtons at reduced rates, for they were turning out to be a couple of rabbits, so to speak. However, he made the best of a bad bargain, and did not once, during the entire interview, stop smiling his professional smile. "Everything seems perfectly normal," he said. "Come back in three weeks for the usual checkup."

The only one who seemed to be really delighted was Miss Kennedy, Dr. Rowland's new nurse. A new nurse was like a cat in a bag, and Claudia's guess was that she wouldn't last very long in Dr. Rowland's exclusive setup. "Yes indeedie," she trilled, when Claudia asked to use the telephone in the outer office. "I just know you want to call hubby and tell him the wonderful news."

Claudia winced. "Yes indeedie" and "hubby" in a single breath. David had a lot to be grateful for. She mightn't be the ideal wife, what with her quick temper and inconvenient susceptibility to pregnancy, but at least she didn't talk too much and what she said was straight and to the point. David was the same way. Good lusty four-letter words became him like an old tweed suit, whereas it would have been blasphemy on his lips to call her "kid," or nickname Bobby "Butch." She wondered, as she dialed his number, what choice morsel of language Dr. Rowland's verdict would elicit from him. He'll probably be terribly moved, and wring my neck, she thought.

It was almost a relief when his secretary said that he'd gone out to see a client, and wasn't intending to return to the office. "I'm sure he didn't expect you, Mrs. Naughton; he planned to drive straight on out to Connecticut from his appointment. I'll try to reach him, but I'm not certain that I can."

"No, that's all right," said Claudia. "I'll make the three o'clock express, and be home ahead of him."

It was too early for the suburban crowds, and she was glad to find an empty section so that she could sit by the window and put her feet up on the opposite seat, without feeling guilty when the conductor came around. Her thoughts were somber. She wished that she could be as happy as she had been when Dr. Rowland had told her about Matthew and Bobby. She felt that she had the right to be happy, and that the new baby had the right to be happy. The new baby had a right to be proud too, because he was going to have David for a father. Men like David ought to have sons, she thought, unashamed for once of being sentimental. But she knew that he was afraid, and she knew also that it was wrong for him to be afraid. If I can only make him realize that his fear is my fear, she thought.

The little Eastbrook station was deserted when she stepped out onto the platform, and a chill drizzle was curtaining the short winter afternoon. It would be a long cold wait if she telephoned Edward to come down for her, and besides it was chore time. She climbed into the one lonely cab, regretting the dollar fare, but pleased because the old man who drove it was so pleased at having a passenger.

The house lay waiting for her in the bend of the road. There were lights in the front windows, she could see them from the top of the hill. Odd, because Jane was usually in the kitchen at this hour, giving Matthew his supper. Then she saw that there was a car before the door. It was a gray coupé with Dr. Barry's initials on the license plate. Her heart jumped into her throat.

She stumbled out of the cab and ran up the walk, afraid to think. The front door stuck, proud with age. She flung herself against it, and it gave to her weight.

There was no one in the living room. She followed the lights upstairs to the nursery. Bobby was in bed and Dr. Barry was bending over him, listening to his chest.

He looked up as she ran in. "Don't be upset, Mrs. Naughton," he said kindly. "It's nothing very serious."

"I have the flu," Bobby enlarged with an interesting croak. "The teacher sent me home from school."

Dr. Barry removed the stethescope from his ears, and answered her unspoken fear. "No congestion, lungs perfectly clear. But he'll have to be quiet until this hoarseness disappears."

"I'm so relieved his lungs are all right." Claudia took a big breath and sank down into a chair. A sloppy sneeze from the next room brought her to her feet again. "Who's that?" she demanded.

Jane appeared at the doorway. "It's Matthew," she explained apologetically. "He began to sniffle after you went this morning, and I took his temperature and popped him into bed."

Mutely, Claudia looked to Dr. Barry for verification. "Has he got it too?" she asked in a small voice.

Dr. Barry opened his black bag and withdrew from its well-stocked interior a large bottle of pink pills and a large bottle of green pills. "I'm afraid so," he admitted, as he poured some of each color pill into two small white envelopes. "There's a lot of it around. Matter of fact, I've been laid up myself all week." He sealed one of the envelopes and wrote Bobby's name on it. "Two every three hours." He started to seal the second envelope.

"Matthew can't swallow pills," said Claudia.

"These aren't for Matthew," said Dr. Barry. "They're for Jane."

It was as good a way as any of breaking the news that Jane was the sickest of the lot, with a hundred and three temperature, and a dogged determination to stay on her feet, since there wasn't a nurse to be had to take her place. Claudia felt like Bobby, when David pulled his tooth out with a string—it was over before he knew it. "Any more?" she asked shakily.

"Not at the moment," said Dr. Barry, who may or may not have had a sense of humor. "But see that Jane gets into bed; she's got a wicked looking throat. I'd advise you to move Matthew's crib out of her room. Let him stay in here with Bobby."

Bobby applauded the suggestion loudly. Matthew wasn't very stimulating company, but one could always throw things at him. He settled himself for an enjoyable illness. "Can I have the radio, too?" he demanded.

"Hold your horses," said Claudia.

Fortunately the crib slipped through the doors without having to be taken apart. Matthew enjoyed the ride and found the change of scenery acceptable.

He, too, settled down to an enjoyable illness. "I want a drink of water," he announced. "And some candy," he added optimistically.

"Mrs. Naughton!" Jane called from the next room. "Could you please step in here?"

"Just a minute, everybody," said Claudia pleasantly, "until I slip on an extra pair of feet."

She found Jane sitting on the edge of her bed, wringing her hands in agitation. "I can't let you do this alone," she moaned. "It's too much, with cooking and housework and taking care of three people besides."

"Oh, shut up," said Claudia. "What do you think I am, a lily? Get undressed and stop this nonsense."

"Mother!" Bobby shouted. "Come back, quick! Matthew spilled his water!"

"That's nice," said Claudia.

Half an hour later, she discovered that she hadn't even taken her hat off. "I didn't know you could be like this," said Jane.

"Like which?"

"I thought you'd go all to pieces with the children sick and all."

"So did I," Claudia confessed. "But I find I'm quite a remarkable person." She smiled at Jane. Jane looked oddly pretty, and not too old in her virtuous white nightgown, and her hair in a braid. It was too bad she didn't have a husband. All women should have husbands, Claudia decided, and all couples should have children. It wasn't always a picnic by any matter of means, but it was probably life's smartest capital investment.

She was squeezing orange juice like mad, when she saw the lights of the car head up the back driveway, like giant eyes. She hurried to the terrace door. A few moments later, David's step sounded on the stone flagging. His lips felt cold, and fresh, and hard. "You smell of pipe," she said.

"What's wrong with smelling of pipe?"

"Nothing. I like it."

He sniffed. "You smell like an orange."

"It's not as bad as smelling from peanuts," she defended. "Did you have a hard day?"

"So-so. Where's everybody? The house seems quiet."

"Oh, everybody has the flu," she said cheerfully. "They're all in bed."

He thought, of course, that she was joking. "Well, I'll be damned," he said, when he found out that it was true. He was very sweet, too, the way he went from one bed to another. "You couldn't be more darling," Claudia complimented him, "if they were your best pigs."

He was even sweet about it when they discovered that it was long past supper time—and no supper in the house. "I never ordered a blessed thing," Jane deplored. "My head was off my shoulders."

"It would have been an ass if it wasn't, with a hundred and four fever," said Claudia, throwing in an extra degree for good measure. "Don't worry, we'll find something in the icebox."

The icebox was one of Jane's best points. She always kept it clean and fresh and up-to-date, with no leftovers hanging drearily about in sundry dishes. Claudia took in at a glance exactly what she had to work with. "I'd better send Edward for some chops," she decided.

David peered over her shoulder. "Hey," he said, "you've got eggs and milk and pot cheese. What do you want to bother with chops for?"

"Not for me. For you. Oh, and here's some duck left, and a spot of apple sauce, how clever of them."

It was really quite a presentable meal with the duck better cold than hot, and cream poured into the scrambled eggs to give them personality. "We use cream like millionaires," Claudia gloated. "Live in the city, and you use the top of the bottle, and not too much of that."

"Some day," said David, "you'll really learn to appreciate this farm."

"I appreciate it now," she said. She had been thinking, as she sat there, that it wasn't going to be so very much expense to have a new baby. If they lived in town, they'd probably have to move to a larger apartment, but old houses were used to babies, there was always an extra room; and the big maples on the side lawn meant that she wouldn't have to wheel a perambulator up and down city streets. There'd always be food to eat, too, and wood to keep them warm. She wondered if she could make David understand that. "The land," she went on aloud, "can be awfully good to you, if you'll only let it."

"What's gotten into you to bring around this change?" he asked her curiously.

"That's an extremely personal question," she replied.

She had meant to tell him in bed, not in the kitchen, but he was quick as a flash—or maybe his mind just worked that way. He leaned across the table and caught both her hands in one of his. "I'll break your little neck. . . ." he said.

She had never heard his voice so husky, nor seen his eyes so full of love. She'd been a fool. She knew all at once that his fear was not her fear. It was the other way around.

Four

THE CHILDREN STAYED IN BED FOR A WEEK, AND GOT up looking spindly. They had the polite air of visitors for a day or two, and then they were back to normal. "The flu is as if it never was," said Claudia on the first Sunday morning that she didn't have to get up to give medicines and fix trays. "Let's celebrate," said David. He kissed her, and went back to sleep.

Claudia lay listening to Jane moving about below. Jane had taken inches off her hips since she'd been ill, and Edward had taken to helping her with the dishes at night. It would be awfully nice and save sheets, thought Claudia elliptically.

She would always remember what a lovely Sunday it started out to be. They hung around the fire in the living room after breakfast, as if they were on a house party. "Edward says," David mentioned, as he puffed his pipe into a light, "that Majesty's daughter is milking thirty-three pounds a day."

"It sounds positively ribald," Claudia commented. "What's it in plain quarts?"

"A little under sixteen," he admitted reluctantly.

"Stick to pounds," she advised. "It's flashier."

His back went up at once. "Pounds or quarts, it's pretty damn good for a heifer," he informed her. "Remember this is her first."

Claudia nodded in agreement. "It's my third," she said mildly, "and I don't expect to do anywhere near that well."

Bobby, who was exercising over the arm of the sofa, froze to attention with his belly halfway to the floor, and his legs pawing the air. There was nothing that he could put his finger on, yet he sensed that there was more to the conversation than met the eye.

"That's just dandy for the couch, what you're doing," said Claudia, anticipating questions. "Get up. Go on. Run and play."

"I have nothing to play," said Bobby.

"How about catching up on a little homework?" David put in.

Bobby got himself right side up without further ado. "I have to fix my airplane," he remembered. He paused at the doorway.

"Can a bull give milk?" he queried thoughtfully. David's high hopes of developing his first-born into a farmer grew less high, for the inquiry definitely lacked flair. "That question is worthy of your mother," he remarked, disgruntled.

"Don't be silly," said Claudia.

"Then what does a bull give?" Bobby persisted. "He has to give something."

"Local color," David told him. "Now, march."

"Don't you think," Claudia asked when they were alone, "that we ought to explain about the baby before he hears it from outsiders?"

"He won't hear it from outsiders if you keep your mouth shut," said David.

She was indignant. "I haven't told a soul. Hardly."

"Talking of bees and flowers, how do you feel?" he digressed.

"I'm glad you think you're a bee. I feel fine. Why?"

"No more dizziness? No more nothing?"

"No more nothing."

"You're a credit to the farm," he said, which was by way of being a very superior compliment. "Do you want to walk up to the knoll and see how it looks now that the brush has been cleared?"

Actually, she wasn't crazy about climbing a hill at that moment, but the least she could do was to live up to his idea of her.

"Let's go before Bobby-the-Censor gets wind of it," she suggested shamelessly.

"Let's," he agreed.

Guiltily, they swung out over the lawn toward the pasture gate. "We're not," said Claudia, "the kind of parents a progressive school endorses. We ought to take him along, and encourage him to call us by our first names, and all be full of merry and eventful chatter."

"The hell we ought," said David.

"I really think you like to be alone with me," she said, being brazenly girlish.

"Sure I do." He paused to chop off the head of a dried thistle with his stick. "And I like the way this field looks too," he added enthusiastically.

"Must I always play second fiddle to a bunch of grass?"

"This is no bunch of grass, lady. This represents ten tons of good alfalfa." He picked up a stone and tossed it into the brook. "These son-of-a-bitch rocks," he muttered.

"I wish you were as tidy in the house," she observed. Newspapers on a carpet never bothered him, but let him cross a meadow, and he'd clear off every weed and stone within his vision.

"And I wish I had the cash to buy the sixty acres adjoining ours," he went on, with the first real envy she had ever heard upon his lips.

"It seems to me," she said, "we've got our hands full with what we've got."

"Yes, but only a quarter of what we've got is tillable," he explained. "What we need is cleared fields to rotate crops."

"I see what you mean," she said, trading honesty for congeniality. "If you really have to have it, Hartley would lend you the money; why don't you ask him?"

"Thanks," he said shortly. "I'm not borrowing."

She rejoiced in the pride that held him rigid, but at the same time, the longing in his eyes as he looked toward the rich meadows beyond their fence line compelled her to temper his abhorrence of debt. "Borrowing from one's own brother is different," she pointed out.

"Thanks," said David again.

"I think you're unfair to Hartley."

"Hartley and I don't talk the same language. Never have."

"I know it. You're as different as different can be. Still, you can't deny that he and Julia are awfully generous to us. I bet they give us a new perambulator for the baby. The one from Bobby's gone to pieces. A third baby's in luck because all the stuff from the first baby's worn out by the second baby."

"Good Lord," he said, "are we back to babies again?"

She drew to a stop, searching his eyes in sudden misgiving. "David, I thought you were really glad that we're going to have another child?"

"Yes, darling," he said soberly, "I'm glad enough, but it's a rotten dirty world to bring a youngster into."

She wooed him with his own gods. "How can you stand here and say that? Look down there at all our beautiful land, and smell our own wood burning, and watch the wind blowing through our own trees—"

"Not one damn bit of it is ours," he said. "Not while madmen roam the earth."

"That's silly," she denied hotly. "It's all ours. Nothing and no one can ever take it away from us!"

He looked at her strangely. "You're funny," he said. "But maybe that's fine. Maybe that's the simple sanity this cockeyed universe needs."

She wanted to deny that she was as simple as she sounded, but she was wise enough to know that simplicity was her strongest ally. It was the only weapon she could use against the burning fury that came so often to snatch the tranquility from his eyes. "David! Be happy," she implored.

"I'm happy," he said.

"Kiss me."

He kissed her. She felt him come to life with passion and completeness. She knew no shame. Her wiles were grounded deep in the very fabric of their marriage, and they were at once her power and her heritage. "Let's talk about a name for the baby," she said a little breathlessly.

"Daniel," he offered promptly.

She snorted.

"What's wrong with Daniel?"

"Show a little fairness, and think up a couple of girls' names for a change."

"It'll be another boy. We're the sort who have sons," he averred with smugness.

"Nevertheless, I know a lot of nice people who have daughters," she argued. "What about Margaret?"

"Why just Margaret?"

"No particular reason. Care for Bridget or Mary?"

He put up his nose.

"I thought you liked plain names."

"Not when they're so plain they're fancy." He drew to a stop. "Look darling," he said gently, "wouldn't you like to call her after your mother?"

She shook her head, unable to talk above the sudden tears that choked her throat. It was a year and a half since her mother had died, and sometimes the missing of her was gone completely, and sometimes it came upon her with a longing that was anguish. Often, when she went to New York she'd manage to pass the pleasant old-fashioned apartment where her mother had lived, stealing a moment from the past to make her own again. It was wrong, and she knew it—wrong to David and the children and herself. Some day she would be strong enough to cut the cord that bound her to her childhood, but not yet. She wondered how much David divined of this secret struggle with herself. They seldom talked of it, but once in a while he would press her hand and she would know that he was aware of the heartache tearing through her; and once in a while he voiced her loneliness, so that it might not grow into a barrier between them. He'd said, when he'd first heard about the baby, "It's tough not having Mother here." And now he said, "I think it'd please her if we named the youngster for her."

"No it wouldn't, it'd bore her to death," said Claudia with a handsome disregard of accuracy as well as sentiment. "Besides, Hannah is a terrible name to burden a child with."

He looked relieved. "We might lop off some of the aitches and fix it up a little," he suggested.

"You're sweet," she said gratefully. "Thanks just the same."

They walked on for a few yards in silence. They came to a fence. A sheep stuck its head out from behind a tree, and all at once, the whole flock was there. "They look so biblical," said Claudia. She wanted to get close to them, and started to climb the fence. They lost their holy aura and stomped away, swinging their fat sides, and flaunting their prerogative.

"Very lovely manners," said Claudia grimly. But David beamed as if they had presented him with a million dollars. "God, but that's good for the land," he rejoiced.

"You and your land," she said. She reached the top rail. He pulled at her coat. "Come down here! That's a fine thing, climbing fences."

"Nonsense. This baby's going to do what I do, and like it."

"It'll have to do what you do, but maybe it won't like it," he remarked. "It's already had some pretty lively stepping."

"Yes, and Dr. Rowland says we're both wonderful." She stood looking down at him. "You have a lovely scalp," she said. "You've no idea how particular I am about scalps."

He vaulted the fence, and lifted her to the ground from the other side, holding her for a moment close against him. "Why don't I get tired of you," he whispered gruffly.

"I don't know," she said humbly. "I often wonder. Look at those tramps!" she broke off.

He followed her gaze to where the Danes came trotting in at the front gate, back from some forbidden escapade.

"Whose chickens have they got now?" said David.

"I don't think it's chickens this time," said Claudia. "They have the air of somebody's garbage pail."

David whistled to them. The dogs turned toward them, and shot forward, devouring the terrain in leaps and bounds. The fence meant nothing to them. They dissolved and poured beneath it, only to bounce back into bone and sinew.

"Can all dogs do that?" asked Claudia. "Or just ours?"

"Just ours," lied David.

They walked on, with the Danes cavorting ahead of them.

"Puffing?" David asked.

"No," lied Claudia. "I never felt better."

He made her sit down anyway on the great stump of a fallen tree. "This is wonderful," she said, relaxing.

"What's wonderful?"

"Everything."

"Isn't it?" he agreed contentedly.

In a little while she was rested enough to walk on again, and suddenly there was Shakespeare, appearing as always from the depths of nowhere. He pretended not to see them, to have been out taking a stroll, minding his own business. The dogs didn't believe a word of it. "Leave that cat alone!" David commanded sternly.

"This is no privacy," said Claudia happily.

They came at last, all five of them, to the hill that had been cleared of brush.

"Now look at your view," said David proudly.

She caught her breath. "Was it always so beautiful?"

"Yes, but we couldn't see it for the trees."

The whole farm spread before them, perfect and miniature and unreal. She saw Bobby running across the lawn to the barn, looking for them. He seemed lost and somehow incomplete. Her heart went out to him.

"Come up and join us!" she called out. "We're on the hill!"

Suddenly David bent to kiss her. She raised her lips to his. Their love lifted to the skies, and their universe lay below them at their feet.

It was a good Sunday dinner—steak (from the butcher's, thank goodness) and french fried potatoes. "Next year we'll be having our own beef," said David.

"Let's live in the present," said Claudia.

They fought about the tenderloin as usual. David speared the juiciest morsel onto Claudia's plate. "No argument, please, I like it tough."

"Now please don't begin that business again; I like it tough too!"

"It's not any of this steak tough," injected Jane, who assumed a personal responsibility for all food brought to the table.

"There!" they triumphed in a single breath.

In the end neither of them would touch it, and Jane, well pleased with the impasse, carried the tenderloin back to the kitchen to be used the following day for Matthew's lunch.

"If there's one thing I can't abide in a person it's a petty streak," Claudia flung at him, though secretly she adored him for not taking it.

"And I can't stand stupidity," he replied. "You ought to have enough sense to realize that you're eating for two."

Bobby looked up from the bone which he always

cleaned up before the dogs got it. "Two what?" he asked. "How can a person eat for two?"

Jane returned from the kitchen with the vegetables in time to hear the question, and got red spots all over her neck in place of blushing. Claudia took pity on her and changed the subject. "Bobby, help yourself to a decent portion of squash," she adjured him.

Bobby was easily sidetracked into squash, which he detested. He made a deal. "I'll take more potato."

"Squash," said David in a sepulchral voice.

"You didn't take any."

David smiled blandly. "Didn't I? I must have overlooked it."

"You never take squash," said Bobby, rebelliously.

David made a clean breast of it. "All right, so I never take squash. What are you going to do about it?"

There wasn't anything that Bobby could do about it. Smoldering with the injustice of it all, he suffered Jane to serve him, and stabbed a load of the hateful mess onto his fork. By some amazing sleight-of-hand, the fork was empty by the time it reached his lips, but he perfected the illusion by gulping a huge swallow of milk to wash it down.

Claudia punctured his fool's paradise. "That isn't going to get you any place," she remarked.

Tortured, Bobby loaded the fork again, and stuffed a sizable portion of the vegetable into his mouth with a great shiver. "You're pretty," said David disapprovingly.

"Also, we know it's in your cheek," Claudia mentioned.

"Children in Europe are starving," David continued.

"That's absolutely true," Claudia followed up.

Bobby fidgeted. The trend of the conversation was growing familiar and unanswerable. There was nothing to do but wolf the squash, and stuff a piece of bread into his mouth to take the taste away. "How does a person eat for two?" he persisted thickly.

"Oh, dear," said Claudia.

"He's got your one-track mind," said David.

"Well anyway, you made the remark to begin with, so you finish it."

David cleared his throat, and squared himself in his chair. "Look here, son—" he began.

"You're the image of a citizen," Claudia murmured.

"All right, you tell him," said David, smarting under the subtle barb.

"Oh no, you were doing fine," she encouraged him. "Go ahead."

He got off to a fresh start, and went straight to the point, without benefit of botany. "How would you like a new baby brother, Bobby?"

"Or a baby sister?"

"Like Matthew?" Bobby enquired with disinterest.

"Well—more or less," said Claudia judicially.

Bobby considered the prospect. "A boy in school has a raccoon," he countered hopefully.

"So you'd rather have a raccoon," said David. "Now suppose we see if we can get some news on the radio."

Bobby jumped up. "I'll do it! I know how to find it!"

"Do you think he's a nitwit, or just pure?" Claudia whispered between screams of static and jazz.

"With his maternal background, it's an even bet," said David. He raised his voice above the din. "Shut it off, Bobby, and come back. I guess there's nothing on now."

"That's good," said Claudia. It was a relief to finish a meal without the intrusion of some smooth voice advertising the merits of chewing gum and the horrors of war in a single breath. She had always been weak in geography and history, and the raging battles in the world were like a lesson that was never finished.

"Where is Bengasi again?" she had asked at dinner the night before.

"Bengasi was, and always will be, exactly where it is," replied David, who abhorred a slovenly intellect.

"That's a big help."

"Bengasi is on the Gulf of Sidra, Cyrenaica," he'd told her, with a long-suffering air.

"That's an even bigger help," she'd said bitterly. "I mean, is it in Asia, Africa, Egypt, or *where?*"

"Don't you listen, for God's sake?"

"I listen and I hear, but it doesn't stay with me," she'd admitted miserably. "One foreign name sounds like another especially if it's more than two syllables."

Today she was relieved that he wasn't so compulsive as usual about the news. He delighted Jane by accepting a second helping of apple pie, after which he lit a cigar instead of his pipe. Bobby recognized the mellow aftermath of Sunday dinner. "Let's play a game of checkers, Dad," he suggested with a lordly quality.

"It's Daddy's one day of rest," Claudia objected.

"Later I will," David promised him.

Bobby eyed them darkly. "Are you going to go to bed again? Every Sunday afternoon you go up and go to bed."

"We don't go to bed," Claudia made clear. "We just lie down and relax."

"Anyway, what's it to you?" David wanted to know.

"I have nothing to do," said Bobby, in what may or may not have been an irrelevancy.

"Have you written Aunt Julia, thanking her for the game she sent you for the flu?" Claudia suggested.

"No," said Bobby. "Can I go out on the road with my bicycle?"

"No," said David.

"Can I go on the pond and ice skate?"

"No," said Claudia.

In the end, he sat down at the desk in the living room to write the letter, breathing heavily with effort.

"Don't bite the tip of your tongue off," Claudia cautioned, as they passed him on the way upstairs.

Bobby looked up. "What's the date today?" he asked.

"December seventh," David called back from the steps.

He didn't stay at the letter very long. In a little while, they heard him at the piano, composing eloquent discords, full of pedal.

"Must he do that?" queried David.

"I think so," said Claudia. "Julia's very musical, remember."

"Julia's no blood relation."

"Even so," said Claudia.

They were aware, after a time, that the piano was quiet. "It's wonderful. Like not having a toothache," said Claudia. She sighed happily. "When the baby comes, it'll be even noisier."

David got up on his elbow, and gazed down at her. His voice held ridicule, but it was tender as a lovesong. "The mother of three," he said. "It makes me laugh."

She was glad that her body remained young and fresh, and in his eyes both lovely and desirable. "I could have a dozen children," she told him, "and you'd always come first." She put her arms around him and drew him down to her, and the years rolled away, and they were lovers that had not met before.

The telephone rang—two long, one short. "That's not us," said Claudia drowsily.

"If it were, I wouldn't answer," David said. "Oh, hell," he broke off. "There's no rest for the wicked, here comes the detective."

"Just lie still and make believe we're asleep," said Claudia, as the sound of Bobby stumbling over himself reached her ears. "If he ever didn't run, I'd take his temperature and call the doctor," she whispered.

He bumped into the table outside their door. It chattered on its legs. "It didn't fall over," he placated himself and them.

They lay perfectly quiet, with closed eyes.

"Mother! Daddy!" he called urgently from the threshold.

"Go away, we're asleep," David mumbled.

"You're not! You couldn't talk if you were asleep!"

"Go away anyway," said Claudia. Then her heart misgave her. If she kept on putting David first, the children would grow up and have psychoses. "What is it, dear?" she asked. "What's bothering you?"

"Nothing," said Bobby.

"For goodness sake," she protested, feeling that her maternal gesture had gone to waste.

"Edward's listening to the radio in his room," Bobby continued.

"Fine," David interrupted. "Join him. He won't mind."

"I did, I was," said Bobby. "He told me to tell you something. That's what I came up for."

"Well, tell," said David. He made a foolish face and Bobby giggled. He giggled so much that he couldn't talk, and ended up with hiccoughs.

"Come, come," Claudia demurred. "Your father isn't as funny as all that. Speak your piece and off with you."

Bobby gave a final hiccough. "Edward said I should tell you that the radio says that Japan attacked Hawaii."

Claudia stretched luxuriously. "That's too bad," she said. But David leaped to his feet, and before they knew what had happened, he was charging down the steps to the living room.

"Well, that's a very odd way for him to act," said Claudia. "Say it over again, Bobby, what you just said."

Bobby repeated his statement with a self-conscious smirk of importance.

"It doesn't make sense," said Claudia, yawning. "Hawaii belongs to the United States, doesn't it?"

Bobby was by no means certain of the answer, but he was nonetheless flattered by her assumption that he knew. He nodded sagely.

"Then," Claudia concluded brusquely, and with

some annoyance, "you misunderstood Edward, and got Daddy upset, for no good reason."

"I didn't," Bobby contradicted. "That's what Edward said: 'Japan attacked Hawaii.'"

"They couldn't," said Claudia.

"Why?"

In turn she found herself gratified by being in the unique position of knowing more about the war than someone else. "Because," she explained a little pompously, "we're a neutral nation. We're not fighting with Japan. The last I heard Japan was making peace with us."

"They attacked us anyway," said Bobby stubbornly. "It's on the radio."

"Don't be silly," said Claudia. "Run down and tell Daddy his manners leave much to be desired."

She waited a few minutes. David would doubtless get the impact of the message and come bounding upstairs again. She waited in vain. With a sense of having been rudely jilted for a rumor, she decided to go in search of him. She paused at the mirror to run a comb through her hair, observing her reflection with approval. Sundays certainly agree with me, she thought.

She found him in the living room. He was bent over the radio. Edward was huddled beside him. The agitated rhythm of some momentous communique filled the air to bursting, but the words carried no significance to her. She was aware only that David's jaw had turned to granite, and that Edward's rugged Vermont face looked pallid beneath the heavy burn of weather. Neither of them knew that she was there, and for a fleeting instant she had the sense that they were not there either, that only empty bodies crouched before her. She felt frightened all at once; she felt that they had been carried off to where she could not follow.

"David!"

He started at the sound of her voice, and straightened slowly. His spirit came back into his face from a long distance away. He said, "It's our war now, darling. We're in it up to our necks."

She stared at him, realizing suddenly that it was not fear, but knowing, that had stalked his days.

"I don't understand," she faltered.

"We're going to get bombed," Bobby lucidly interpreted. He appeared to find the idea agreeable, and draped himself across the sofa, and airily waved his legs.

"Bobby, get up," said Claudia mechanically.

"Such talk. Bombed indeed," Jane scoffed from the doorway of the dining room. Nevertheless she bent swiftly and lifted Matthew in her arms. He kicked his fat knees into her stomach. "I want to get down!" he asserted.

"Come on, Matthew, let's play," said Bobby. The war had abruptly lost its novelty, while Matthew, who had no possessiveness and some new toys from his Aunt Julia, offered more immediate entertainment.

"Mind you're not rough," Jane cautioned. She did not follow them as her usual good sense would dictate. She just went on standing in the doorway, listening, with her lips in a thin, straight line. She did not even remember it was suppertime until Matthew reappeared, a little the worse for wear, and said, "I'm tired. I want my supper." "Poor lamb!" she cried contritely. "Jane's coming right this instant."

Edward said, "I have to go too. It's time for chores."

David turned the radio off. The war receded, and there was stillness. Claudia switched on the lights. Edward was the first to speak. He said, "They shouldn't ought to have done it. They're yellow rats, and now we've got to wipe them off the earth." He said it with a grief that was as strong as might. Then he stared down at his right hand that had been crippled by a saw. "Maybe they won't take a man who hasn't got but four fingers on his hand to fight with," he said.

Claudia cried swiftly, "You won't have to fight, Edward; you have children to take care of!"

It was as if he hadn't thought of his children. "They're all right," he said, slowly. "They're all right with their grandmother. The important thing is they have to have a decent world to live in."

David said, "You stay with the land, Edward.

That's important, too. We'll need men on the land."

A band of ice unwound itself from Claudia's heart. She breathed again. "Of course we'll need men on the land, Edward. Don't be silly."

They waited until he had gone out before they spoke again. "Poor devil," David said.

"Poor devil, why? Because he has children to provide for?"

David looked at her strangely. He didn't say anything.

"You told him yourself he ought to stay with the land!" she reminded him with fear catching hold of her anew.

"I said it because they won't take him anyway."

"His hand?"

"Yes, and his teeth. And his eyes aren't any too good either."

She laughed shakily. "I fell in love with your hands. And you can read the telephone directory in the dark. And your teeth are stunning."

"Are you sorry?" he asked quietly.

"I don't know."

She went to the window. Darkness had blotted out the neatly fenced fields and rolling meadows, and somewhere beyond the darkness there was bloodshed and destruction. The battle that was raging was no longer a remote page of history; it was happening now, to her own people. She could not make herself realize it, for she had never lived through a war before. She hadn't been as old as Bobby in the last war, and it had become a legend in the years between. Gasless Sundays, and cakes without sugar. Such little things to give up. "Dear God, I'll do anything, suffer anything, only don't let David go!" Even if they were bombed, her mind raced on, it wouldn't matter as long as they were all together. Her heart began to pound against her ribs, and the palms of her hands turned clammy. What was she afraid of? Of course they'd be together. David wouldn't go—he couldn't go. There was the new baby. For a moment, she had forgotten about the new baby. Her heart stopped pounding. The new baby dictated David's course of action as surely as Edward's crippled hand made certain his rejection. There was nothing to be afraid of. She turned back into the room, with courage supplanting fear.

David was filling his pipe. She always liked to watch him—he was so comfortable and leisurely about it. Now, however, his fingers were tense and jerky as he tamped the tobacco in the bowl, and his eyes were gray instead of blue. She couldn't see through them to what was going on inside his thoughts. She wanted to say something, but she was barren of words. It was wrong that they should be apart at a time like this. She tried to recapture the joyous oneness of the afternoon. It was gone. They were separate entities, inimical and impenetrable.

"David—" she began in a desperate effort to break through to him.

"What?" he swiftly asked.

She reached into her mind, but she could find nothing worthy to bring forth. He did not press her. She went back to staring out of the window into the blackness. She thought, It's because we're so close that we're suddenly apart. We don't know how to be dishonest with each other.

Jane came back into the room. "I put a bite of supper on the table," she said in a hushed tone, as if a death had disrupted the robust tenor of the household.

They sat down, but they weren't very hungry. "I was never mad about an omelette anyway," Claudia apologized.

"You don't have to be mad about it," said David. "Remember, you're eating for two," he added with a faint smile.

"I thought you'd forgotten it," she said lightly.

"No. I hadn't forgotten it," he replied. He rose and turned the radio on. The war marched in on them again. It came in through the closed door of the kitchen, where Edward too, sat listening as he ate his supper. Jane herded the children off to bed, a brief interlude of normalcy.

"I'm glad they're little!" Claudia cried defiantly. At least it wasn't a lie. She felt cleaner after she had said it.

David remained silent for a space. Then he said, "Of course you're glad. You wouldn't be human if you weren't."

She wondered, rebelliously, if he expected her to be more than human. It wasn't fair. He had no right to command her beyond the potential of her being.

"Do you want another cup of coffee?" she asked in lieu of conversation.

"If it's there."

"It's here. Cream? Sugar?"

He nodded. "That's fine," he said.

Constraint settled again between them. It was a relief when the telephone bell rang. She hurried to answer it.

"Long distance!" she called back to him. "I think it's Hartley."

She was still on the wire when David picked up the receiver in his study.

"Well—" said Hartley, clearing his throat.

David cleared his throat too. "Rotten mess," he said.

There was a long pause. Claudia wanted to ask for Julia, but it was not easy to interrupt their silence, for in that silence, they were more deeply brothers than they had ever been before. They might not have said another word, and yet she had the sense that they had told each other, in a kinship that surpassed the accident of birth, all that could be said. Perhaps that was happening at this moment all over the world, people

finding one another in the common outrage of a rav-
ished decency and faith. It was a moment of com-
munion that should have been theirs alone. Claudia
felt herself an eavesdropper on their screaming
thoughts. She had to let them know that she was
there.

"How's Julia?" she managed to bring out at last.

"Julia's gone," said Hartley.

"Gone where?" she asked in a single voice with
David.

"Getting soldiers back to camp. She'll be out all
night."

"Oh," said Claudia. She remembered that Julia had
been on a committee for volunteer service. David always said that if you cut Julia open you'd find com-
mittees instead of organs, and intellect instead of
brains, and ideas instead of feelings. Yet for all of that
—perhaps because of it—Julia was the first of them to
function. Hartley felt it and wore the hurt of it like
a wound. "God," he said, "if I were only ten years
younger."

"I'm ten years younger," David answered with a
tinge of bitterness, "but what good does it do me?"

Hartley understood what David had left unsaid.
He cleared his throat once more. "Look here, I can
take care of your family, but you can't take care of
my blood pressure."

"That's right," said David; and then after a long,
hard pause, he humbly added, "Thanks."

Claudia slowly hung the receiver back upon its hook. *Thanks*. The word carried an echo, tantalizing and disturbing. Then she remembered that that morning, when they'd been talking about the land adjoining theirs, she had said to him, "Let Hartley lend you the money," and David had answered shortly, "Thanks." How differently it sounded now upon his lips, as if something bigger than pride had come into his life and made him humble. She felt the power of that something, and she was frightened and bewildered by its immensity. She ran upstairs in an impulse to surround herself once more with the small, sweet world that spelled her security and her happiness.

The door of the children's room stood open. Cold air was blowing in from the windows, but their hands were warm outside the covers. They were sweet and helpless as they lay there sleeping, and suddenly they were not only her children, they became all children. She thought, What Edward said is true. The world must be kept a decent place for them to live in. Her mind told her that, but her heart could not feel it. Her heart could only feel that somewhere, somehow, there had been some ignoble error in the universe; but it was not her error, and she was unwilling to pay the price to make it right.

"I'm awake," Bobby mumbled, to show he wasn't missing anything.

"No you're not."

"I am so, I want a drink," he said. But he didn't

really, and before he finished saying it, he was off to
sleep again.

She found Edward in the bedroom, laying the fire
for the morning. He did not hear her come in. She
stood in the shadows, watching him. His hands were
slow, and fumbled a little, as if his mind were not on
the task that he was doing. When he rose, he gave a
great sigh, that seemed to come from deep within
him. Claudia felt, as she had felt over the telephone,
that she was an intruder upon this special kind of pain
that came to men who could not fight. Hartley and
Edward and David. They were all three of them
brothers, unified by a single urge that was as old as
life. David was the most fortunate of these three, for
he was the strongest and the ablest. She must not try
to harness him to incapacity, she must not paralyze
his manhood with her righteous hold on him. It
would avail her nothing. War came into her heart,
and tore it open.

She was in her nightgown, standing before the mirror combing her hair, when David came upstairs. He
moved toward her and stood with his head against
hers. "We're a pretty handsome couple," he remarked.

She loved him for the clumsy overture; he was not
going to make her pay for the blistering agony in his
soul. "Not 'pretty', 'very'," she rejoined in kind. But
she was thinking how strange it was that their reflections had not changed—they both looked just as they

had looked that morning when they'd started for the knoll. Perhaps, when the war was over, they would return to those reflections, and find them waiting to be reclaimed. But for the present there was a dirty job that had to be cleaned up. Men would accomplish it in one way, and women in another. It was not too soon to begin. Only she must work toward her own ends in her own fashion.

"Look," she said, "this is going to be hard on my type of female."

"What is?"

"The war."

She could feel him tense. "Take Julia, for instance," she continued.

"I wouldn't," he injected. "Not for a gift."

"Don't say that. You'll be surprised how becoming the war will be to her. She's going to blossom in it, be things and go places."

David grinned.

"But the war's not going to do one thing for me but bring out my defects," she went on gloomily. "I won't even be good at rolling bandages."

"And worse at knitting socks," he agreed.

She bridled a little. "But I could drive an ambulance!"

"Heaven forbid," he said. "You stay home and have your baby and that'll be sufficient contribution from your end, young lady."

She bent forward to examine an imaginary moustache on her upper lip. "Oh it won't take me long to have the baby, having a baby is nothing. Especially with Jane and Edward here."

He quirked an eyebrow. "And where do I come in?"

"Darling, you have," she said demurely. "We won't need you around the place for quite a while again."

"Hey," he said. "What are you talking about?" He looked a little self-conscious, just the way Bobby always did, when something nice was aimed in his direction.

"Although," she went on, half to herself, "there probably won't be much use for architects, I suppose."

"The hell there won't! How do you think we're going to establish bases?"

"Just what are bases?" she asked, carefully using only the top part of her voice.

"Nobody ever teach you any history? Hawaii's a base. Alaska's another."

Her spirit swooned. "I get the general idea," she broke in. Her nails dug deep into her palms. "Would you be wearing a uniform?"

"Certainly I would," he swaggered, now looking completely like Bobby. "With my training, I'd be a lieutenant right off the bat."

"And I'd be proud enough to bust," she said.

He drew her to him. She could scarcely breathe for the way he held her. Strange. She had let him go, and yet he had never been more close. He was close to her even after he had gone downstairs. "I can't get to sleep for a while," he told her. "You go to bed. I'll be up soon."

It wasn't long before she heard the radio again. She knew that if she went downstairs, she would find his empty body, with his spirit far away. It did a woman no good to keep an empty body. All women on this night had lost their men, whether they were aware of it or not. She was one of thousands. There was no nobility in the gesture of letting David go. There was not even patriotism in her heart. She realized, simply, that she could not hold him.

Perhaps, in time, she might rise to greater heights. Suffering might lend her stature, and loneliness give place to the exaltation of having served. But for the moment, she could feel only blind rebellion, and it was her prerogative as a wife and mother to cry out her violent protest against bloodshed and destruction. It might come to pass that in the weeks and months and years ahead God would show His hand in some divine pattern of His making. But now, in this hour of her soul's new agony, she could glimpse no reason for this vicious waste of life. She bit her lips to keep her sobs from rising.

It was hours later that she heard David's step upon the stairs. She felt him standing by the bed.

"Claudia—" he said softly.

She made her breathing deep and regular, so that he would not know she was awake. She had made him free. She must not let her tears become a chain to hold him.

Five

NOTHING HAPPENED FOR WEEKS AND WEEKS. THEN one evening she called for him at the station and she knew at once, from the way he clowned across the platform, that he had news for her. The more bow-legged he walked, the surer she became.

"What's wrong?" she demanded suspiciously.

"Nothing's wrong. On the contrary. Slide over."

"On the contrary, how? I'll drive."

"No Ma'am. Go on slide. Or I won't tell you. How's everything home?"

"Fine. Hurry up. Don't keep me in suspense."

"Electrician come?"

"You make me want to scream! Yes. It was a defective cable, he'll fix it tomorrow. Now tell me!"

"Say 'please'."

She clenched her fists. "Please."

"Nicely," he reproved her.

"Nicely," she whimpered.

He steered with one hand and then no hands, as he lit a cigarette.

"If I did that," she said, "I'd never hear the end of it."

"You bet you wouldn't."

"David, if you don't tell me, I'll open this **door and jump**."

"Tell you what?"

She wished that her pride was stronger than her curiosity, but it wasn't. "Whatever it was you had to tell me," she replied stiffly.

He pretended surprise. "Oh, I thought I did tell you. I passed my physical. I'm the perfect specimen of American manhood."

She could only say, "Oh," with her tongue going dry and swollen against the roof of her mouth. All along she had been hoping against hope that one very small little bodily defect would fail to meet the particular standard of army requirements. Nothing serious, she'd been quick to impress upon some invisible chairman of human fate—nothing like lungs or heart or kidneys. "Flat feet. Or color blindness. Or even hemorrhoids," she'd thrown in recklessly. She didn't know anything about hemorrhoids first hand, but Roger had them, and from what she gathered they could be very painful without being in the least dangerous—certainly an inconvenient background for a soldier, and the ideal thing for David to have had. But no—he had to go and be perfect from top to bottom.

"Are you sure they examined you all over?" she queried with one last ray of hope. "Feet and eyes and everything?"

"Feet and eyes and everything," said he. "Nothing to worry about."

"Nothing to worry about," she echoed bitterly. "Couldn't you have had just a little something wrong with you? Like Roger?"

"That's a nice wifely thought."

"It's better than getting shot."

"A fine patriot you turned out to be."

"Women aren't born to be patriots. It's against nature. What happens now that you've passed your physical?"

"I wait."

"For what?"

"More red tape."

"I hope there's reams of it."

"There will be. It might be a matter of days or months before I'm inducted."

"That's going to be wonderfully relaxing. Where will you have to go?"

"Anywhere they send me."

"Who's they?"

"Now who do you think 'they' is?—Look, what have you been doing to the car, I don't like the way it's acting."

"I took it out today and bit it.—David, suppose they send you to Persia."

"Why Persia?"

"It said something over the radio today—"

"I wish you'd stop listening to the radio," he interrupted. "You just get yourself worked up over nothing. For all you know, I'll be stationed right here."

Her heart leaped. "Right here where?"

"Boston, Washington, New York. I don't know. Right here."

"Who said so?" she inquired breathlessly.

"Nobody said so. It stands to reason. We need airdromes and defense plants in this country, as well as overseas."

"I never thought of that."

"But I'll go where I'm sent. I'm no different than anyone else."

"That's where you're wrong!" she burst out. "Do you realize that not one married man in this whole town has enlisted? And some of the single men that have been drafted have been trying to get out of it? It makes me boil."

"Where did you pick up that pretty bit of gossip?"

"I met Nancy Riddle marketing."

David's dislike of Nancy flared anew. "What's she doing up here this time of the year? Afraid New York's going to be bombed?"

"She always keeps her house open," said Claudia, making no issue of Nancy's frailties. "Anyway, she said she couldn't understand why you should volunteer, with two children and another coming."

"Maybe it's because I have two children and another coming."

"All right, what about other men with families?"

"That's their problem," said David, with neither rancor nor smugness. He pulled up on the side of the road and turned off the motor. "Better let's talk this thing out, or it'll get to be a sickness in your soul."

"It is already," she admitted miserably. "Every once in a while I can take it, and every once in a while I can't. I hate war. I hate it! I hate it!"

"You're not supposed to like it, you cluck."

She laughed shakily. "Oh, well that's different, you should have told me before. Come on, start the car, we have to hurry."

"Why?"

"We're having broiled lobster for supper. Are you happy?"

"Very happy." He drew her to him. "I adore broiled lobster," he whispered.

They passed Elizabeth Van Doren's house on the way home. It wore the clean, unlived-in look of a new building. The lawns were freshly graded, and the shrubbery young and awkward, and not yet part of the landscape to which it had been transplanted.

"Shall we stop for a minute?" David asked. They had gotten into the friendly habit of dropping in on her now and again, but tonight Claudia was glad of an excuse to drive straight on. "I telephoned her earlier; she's gone to New York on some legal business about her husband's will." The words were hard to say. She shuddered as she spoke them. Elizabeth was lucky, in a way—her future was behind her. Life could deal her no greater blow than she had already suffered.

Bobby was waiting for them, his nose buttoned against the windowpane. He was already in his pajamas, having been bathed, scrupulously and against his will, by Jane who had also washed his hair, and slicked it off his forehead.

"You look like a peeled onion," said Claudia, and immediately ruffled it up. Bobby clutched at the ruins of what had been a flat sleek pompadour. "You spoiled it!" he cried accusingly. "Jane's training my hair like Daddy's!"

"Oh, dear," said Claudia. "Can't she find something else to do?"

"Mama wants us to be sissies," David sympathized. "She doesn't want you to grow up, and she doesn't want me to go to war."

Bobby was quick to read between the lines. "Did they take you?" he asked eagerly.

"Yop."

"Whoopee!" said Bobby.

Claudia felt strangely bereft, conscious of a vast companionship between her son and husband that she could never share. They understood each other and they spoke the same language. She knew herself at this moment to be a poor soldier, and turned away lest they glimpse the unreadiness of her spirit, and despise her for it.

She hurried upstairs to Matthew. Jane was just lifting him out of the tub. He hadn't outgrown his potbelly and his curls were a baby-gold. Claudia buried her face in his fat neck. He was something real to hold on to in a distorted world.

She was grateful for the diversion of a lobster supper. Lobsters were expensive, but Jane obligingly got a rash from shellfish, and Edward preferred pork chops, which made lobsters quite economical after all. It was a messy meal, with nutcrackers, and a flock of paper napkins, and finger bowls for purely functional purposes. Bobby sat with a large confusion of amputated legs in front of him and chewed air, blissful in the erroneous impression that he was imbibing heavily of an indigestible and grown-up food.

"Here," said David, magnanimously donating two small crimson flanks of tail off his own plate.

Bobby was mute with gratitude.

"Dear generous Daddy," Claudia murmured.

Jane, jealous of any festivity that excluded Matthew, brought him down in his pajamas, and put him in his high chair. Immediately he reached businesslike hands toward Bobby's pile of lobster legs. Bobby cupped them protectingly. "You can't have any, you're too little."

" 'Twon't hurt him," said Jane, and chose a meatless spike, and gave it to him. He didn't like the taste of it, and threw it to the floor. Shakespeare, who was biding his time beneath the table, slithered off with it in low-slung stealth. The dogs raised a perfunctory opposition, since fish was not their especial dish, and then went back to being in everybody's way. This is a madhouse, thought Claudia, with her heart bursting. She looked around the room as if to print it indelibly on her vision. Unlike most dining rooms, it was uncluttered and serene. The two old low-boys boasted a single bowl apiece for flowers, and a pair of knife boxes flanked the Sheraton sideboard which might have been a priceless antique if they hadn't shared the guilty secret that it was merely fashioned of old wood.

"I like this room, it's graceful," Claudia suddenly remarked, out of a yearning to hold everything exactly as it was now, forever.

"I like it too," said David.

Neither of them voiced what they were thinking—that the room was a symbol of their being a family, and that thousands and thousands of families must be sitting around their dining-room tables, wondering how much longer they would remain together. Then the thought came to her that there were thousands of families who would never know the cruel disruption of war, there were men in this very town who were willing to enjoy the freedom that others died for. Perhaps, she thought resentfully, mankind was not worth the saving. Perhaps David's quixotic gesture would go for nothing in a cause that was already lost.

"You're not eating your lobster," David noticed.

"Yes I am."

"I want a real piece," Bobby demanded.

Claudia clucked her tongue. "Of all the rank ingratitude, with literally hundreds of legs!"

"But there's nothing in the legs," he protested, with an air of having uncovered one of life's major disillusionments.

She knew how he felt. She felt that way herself; she leaned over and kissed him.

"Can I have some more?" he followed up hopefully.

"You certainly mayn't," she said.

"Cheer up, Bobby," David sympathized. "I've been putting up with that kind of thing for years."

Bobby looked immensely gratified at this new adult bond that had sprung up between them. The lobster was no longer important. "I think I'll smoke a cigarette," he said.

David offered him one. He took a puff and choked on it. "Enough is enough," said Claudia.

"He's a nice youngster," David remarked, after they had left the table and Bobby had gone to bed.

Claudia nodded. She could not speak. What they were both savoring was the simple perfection of the world that lay within their own four walls. People like David and herself did not ask for war, they wanted only to go on living their quiet inconspicuous lives. "It's unfair!" she cried.

He looked up from his pipe. "What is?"

"War. What do you suppose 'what is'? What is it that anyone talks or thinks about these days? It's always there in the back of your mind."

"That's your mistake," he said. "You have to go on living just as if."

"As if," she mocked harshly. "As if you weren't going to go away. As if we mightn't be separated next month, or maybe next week. Or maybe even tomorrow."

"There's only today," said David. "And that's as much as there ever is."

"Philosophy," she scoffed.

"What's wrong with philosophy?"

"It's a drug, used chiefly in middle age. The only emotion I'm capable of at this point is rage. Just pure rage."

"That's a pretty good emotion," David commented. "It's enough to win the war. Plus a little faith, and an ultimate belief in man."

"I seem to be lacking the last two requirements." She took the evening paper and sat down in the big chair opposite the sofa. She opened it blindly. She didn't want him to see the despair in her eyes, nor the tears that she was trying to fight off.

The paper backfired at her, as it had a way of doing.

"Oh, God," said David desperately. "Must you?"

"Must I what?"

"I haven't read the editorial yet."

"Don't worry, I'm being particularly careful."

"You're being particularly careful to get the backside front and the frontside back and the inside out."

"That's because you're watching me and making me nervous." She tossed the paper over to him. "Here, take it. I read enough anyway. Another American convoy just landed in Australia."

"Good," said David.

"How can you say that? They might have all been lost."

"Nonsense. Look at statistics."

"I don't want to look at statistics. All I know is that if I had a son—or a husband—" her voice broke a little, "I'd want him to keep off the ocean."

"You don't know what you're talking about. In the last war we didn't lose a single transport carrying troops."

"Thanks."

"And our casualties on the field," he continued, unperturbed, "were no greater than in civilian life."

Claudia made a sound that was halfway between a sob and a snicker. "You talk as if it were as safe to go to war as to fall asleep in your own bed."

"It is," he had the face to tell her.

"I prefer bed for both of us."

"It's only eight o'clock. We can't," he objected. "It isn't done in nice families."

Jane came in at that juncture, with her hat and coat on. "Leaving us?" David inquired amiably.

"She's afraid the new baby's going to be too much work," said Claudia.

Jane laughed. "Edward's going into Bridgeport to pick up the cream separator, and I thought 'twould be a good chance for me to do some shopping."

" 'Twould indeed," said Claudia. She remembered how pretty Jane had looked when she was in bed with the flu, with her hair over the pillow. "Why don't you and Edward go to a movie while you're there?" she suggested.

A faint blush crept over Jane's cheeks as she admitted that the idea had already occurred to them.

"Have a good time!" Claudia called after her. "Don't hurry back!"

"Stop matchmaking," said David.

"Why should I? I think it would be lovely."

"Jane's older than Edward."

"I don't mind that," said Claudia.

"That's big of you," said David. "Let's go to bed."

He managed to invest the proposal with an air of complete originality. She looked prim. "We've just had supper. Nice people don't."

"Who wants to be nice people?"

"I'd like to be nice people," she said wistfully. "I'd like to be able to accept this war with gallantry and fortitude and all the rest of the fine-sounding adjectives you read about."

"I'd as soon be married to a pamphlet."

"It's nice of you not to expect me to be noble. Maybe I'll learn in time. But war is such a new experience," she faltered.

He put his arms around her. "It's new to all of us, darling." For the first time she heard a note of uncertainty in his voice; for the first time she realized that strong men had their moments of struggle, and their weakness was their courage. They clung together, bewildered and lost in a world where human life was negligible. There was no precedent for what was happening to them, no familiar landmarks to hold on to."

"I wish I drank," she said. "If I did, I'd get drunk now."

"I'll fix you a highball."

"I'd rather have a lemonade. Only there aren't any lemons. Anyway I'm not thirsty, I'm just scared."

"Don't be," he said simply.

"I can't help it. Suppose they call you tomorrow? Suppose something happens to you?"

"Then you'd have to take it. The same as thousands of others."

"I couldn't!"

"Look," he said patiently. "We're right back where we started from when I got off the train tonight. How about bed?"

"You're fed up with me," she accused him. "And I don't blame you, I'm fed up with myself." She changed the subject resolutely. "I have a new night-gown. Shall I save it for having the new baby or wear it now?"

"Both," said he.

Out of a perfectly clear sky, he sat up in bed and said, "I smell smoke."

"You smell smoke more than any man I ever knew," she said, with the wind completely out of her sails. "Lie down and don't be silly."

"Don't you smell it?" he insisted.

"No, and if I did, what of it? We left the fire burning in the living room."

"I banked it. And anyway it's not that kind of smell."

"Listen," she called after him, "what's more important, me or smoke?"

"Smoke!" he threw back from the stairs.

She had barely time to be insulted when he came bounding up again. "Claudia! Grab the phone and notify operator there's a fire!"

His voice sounded hoarse and queer in the darkness. She switched on the lamp at her side. This was carrying a joke too far. "Don't be silly," she repeated. Then she saw that he was already prancing into his trousers, and stuffing his pajama coat down inside his belt. "Stop wasting time!" he commanded sharply. "Phone the operator, and then get dressed as fast as you can!"

Still she didn't believe him. "David, this isn't funny," she reproved him, "really it isn't."

"Do as I tell you! Put something warm on, and hurry!"

He was off before she could ask any questions. She picked up the telephone by the bed. "This is Mrs. Naughton, we have a fire," she said, feeling a little foolish about it, particularly since the operator seemed to take it so seriously. She felt like adding, "Don't bother to do anything about it, though, my husband has a complex when it comes to fires." She refrained, however, and, with no great urgency, slipped on a pair of slacks and a sweater.

She was not surprised to find the living room looking just as usual, with the embers glowing harmlessly in the grate, and Shakespeare enjoying an illicit nap on the wing chair. Her sense of quiet maturity heightened as she explored the peaceful order of the dining room and kitchen. "My poor benighted neurotic!" she called out, "where are you?"

He seemed to get the general gist of the query, if not the more subtle implication. "In the cellar!" he yelled back. "Don't come down!"

It was as good as an invitation. She hurried to the cellar door and opened it. Involuntarily she stepped back, for it was as if a blanket of smoke were tossed into her face.

"I told you not to come down!" he shouted up at her. "See if the children are all right!"

She hated to leave him in the middle of so much smoke, but after all there wasn't the remotest sign of flames. It was probably the furnace acting up again. Furnaces were a mystery and a nuisance.

The upper hall seemed fresh and clear after the heavy odor that filled the downstairs rooms. She switched on the lights in the nursery. She sniffed. The smell was stronger in here, there was no doubt of it. It was acrid and penetrating. Matthew was coughing a little, and tossing restlessly in his sleep. Automatically she moved to his side to straighten his blankets. It was then that she noticed a black scorch on the white wall against which the crib was placed. As she looked, it grew larger, and ominously blotted its way toward his head. An instinctive fear swept her belatedly into action. She picked him up, and rushed with him to Bobby's bed. "Bobby! Wake up! You have to get out of here! Quick!" She shook him frantically.

He frowned in his sleep and pushed her away, curling back into the eternal crescent of childhood.

She tried to lift him with her free arm, but he was heavy beyond belief. "Bobby, please!" she implored him. "Open your eyes! Listen to me!"

"You're waking me up," he complained, "go away." He turned his back on her, and pulled the covers over his head, nailing them tightly with his fists.

Panic filled her. The black scorch was spreading,

and she knew without knowing how she knew it, that there wasn't a moment to lose. She carried Matthew down to the living room, and threw him on the sofa, grateful that he kept on sleeping. Then she rushed to the cellar door and clambered down the wooden steps, gagging on the gusts of smoke that stuffed her mouth and stabbed the eyes. For a moment she could not find David, and her knees went boneless until her vision cleared and she saw him chopping at the far wall with an axe. She stood there drenched in horror as a thin red tongue of flame darted out at him like some sly foe crouching for attack. She got to his side somehow. "David! Come quick! Help me get Bobby out of his room!"

He dropped the axe. A groan tore through him. "Oh, God, if it's spread upstairs, it's too late—" He dragged her after him up to the kitchen, and thrust her by main force to the entry. The effort to talk seemed to tear his lungs apart. "Go out on the lawn and stay there!" he gasped. "I'll get the children."

"Don't be silly," she retorted briskly.

The familiar phrase pulled the ghost of a smile across his swollen lips. "Stay put, or I'll knock your fool little block off!"

She made no retort. In the full glare of the light, his face frightened her. It was pallid and covered with thick yellow beads of sweat. "I'll wait," she assured him quickly.

She waited, but only until she heard him on the

floor above. Then she raced after him, throwing a quick glance at the sofa to make certain that Matthew had not wakened. "Childhood's wonderful," she thought.

When he reached the nursery, David was getting Bobby on his feet. He struggled up through layers of sleep, rallying immediately to equality. "What's the big idea!" he swaggered in a deep voice.

"None of your business what's the big idea," David barked back at him. "You're going for a walk."

He swooped up an armful of clothes from a chair and started to untangle them. Claudia whisked them away. "Those are Matthew's, simpleton."

His fingers closed around her arm. "I thought I told you to stay outdoors!"

She pulled free of him. "Shut up, this is my department."

She moved to the closet for Bobby's coat and shoes. Her panic was lifting. The black scorch on the wall had grown no larger, and the smoke in the room was not as noticeable as it had been before. David had lost his head a little, for whatever trouble had started in the cellar was probably dying down. She wondered if it were necessary to get the children out of the house. A March wind was blowing up, and they'd be asking for sniffles, sure as fate. "I think if we left the children quietly in the living room—" she ventured, as she opened the closet door.

The words were crammed back into her throat.

She stifled a scream, and slammed it shut again. She felt as if they had been hunted, and trapped, for the thin red tongue of flame had followed them up here, and was licking its sly way along the closet wall.

She would always remember two things about that night. First, the way Bobby stood, ludicrous and pitiful, with his shoes on the wrong feet, looking up at the cloud of rosy smoke against the gun-metal sky. "Our house is on fire," he said.

The second thing she would remember was the way David bent to kiss her. "I tried to save it for us, darling, but I couldn't."

She lifted her lips to his. "We've saved us. That's all that matters. . . ."

In her heart, however, she knew that this night would leave a scar upon her for as long as she lived. Strange that she had always felt that fires happened to others, but never to oneself. It was something you had to experience, to know. It was a little like being a virgin. Once it happened, you could never go back to being what you were.

She was aware suddenly, that David was gone from her side, and an instant later Bobby broke out into an anguished scream. "Daddy, come back! Don't go in the house again, you'll get burned!"

"I've got to get the dogs out!" David shouted back from the doorway. "Stay with mother!"

Claudia felt a monstrous conflict that was more

nightmare than reality. If only Jane were here to keep watch on the children. "Bobby! Listen to me," she besought him desperately, "can I trust you to take care of Matthew? I have to go with Daddy—"

Bobby's world was crumbling. His voice climbed in terror. "Please, please stay here, Mother! You'll both get burned up!" He clung to her hand and twisted it with all his strength. "I won't let you go! I won't! I won't!"

She knew his desolation, and her heart ached for him. "I have to go, Bobby. The dogs have no collars on, Daddy won't be able to manage them alone. But I can't help him unless you help me by taking care of Matthew."

Matthew understood nothing of what was happening, except that he had been rudely dislodged from his warm bed. He began to cry.

Bobby's jaw stiffened. "Stop being a baby!" he said contemptuously. Dignity settled upon him, and age came into his soul. "You can go and help Daddy," he told her. "I'll watch Matthew."

Claudia looked at him, and knew that she could trust him. He was the projection of David's very being. She gave Matthew's hand into his clasp. "I'll be back," she promised. "We'll both be back."

As she had expected, David was having trouble with the Danes. They wouldn't budge from the soft rug in the passageway outside the kitchen. It was where they always slept, and since they had not committed any undue breach of etiquette, they could see no reason for this premature expulsion into the chill outdoors. David pushed and shoved and cursed at them, but they plastered their huge bodies firmly to the floor, and looked righteous.

"Get some meat!" he shouted, as Claudia rushed to his aid.

She ran back to the kitchen and opened the icebox, damning Jane for the tidiness which made her hide things under covers. There was no time to pick and choose. She grabbed a roast of beef, and tore it from its wrappings.

Smoke cut into her eyes and lungs. She couldn't see for the stinging tears that glued her lids together, she couldn't speak above the pain that slit her chest. She reached for breath. "Here, Bluff! Here, Bluster!"

She gave up a prayer of thankfulness, as the incredible offering electrified them into action. They made a competitive leap for it, only to stop short on the threshold of the smoke-filled kitchen. They backed away distrustfully.

David's face was gaunt. "I was afraid of that," he muttered. He bent, and with a superhuman strength, encircled Bluff's massive struggling body with his arms. Then he lifted him, and staggered to the entry, and pushed him out onto the lawn. Panting, and streaked with soot and sweat, he came back for Bluster; but Bluster would have none of such indignity. He made a dash for freedom.

For an instant Claudia leaned in exhaustion against the door, and watched the dogs disappear into the night. It was a black night, and sparks were flying instead of stars. She heard David make a sound that was prayer and blasphemy combined. "The wind's changed, get back to the children; I'll see if the barn's all right!"

Her strength returned from some hidden source. She ran toward the front of the house, where she could see Bobby and Matthew standing obediently as she had left them, small, motionless silhouettes against the sky. She turned back. Bless them, bless them, bless them—they were giving her the right to follow David. He would need her help, for the barn was full of new-born lambs.

Halfway across the lawn, she remembered Shakespeare. Had he escaped? Or was he still sleeping on the wing chair with death creeping up on him? It was unthinkable. Shakespeare was part of the family. David had bought him for her the first year they were married, a tiny ball of yellow fur that fit into a candy box. By all odds, Shakespeare came before the lambs. She sped back toward the house, a phantom house with its halo of rosy shimmering smoke.

She didn't want the children to see her, so she used the kitchen entrance again. The acid taste of the fumes no longer affronted her lungs or shocked her lips, for she knew how to hold her breath and close her nostrils against it. It made her dizzy, though.

She had to catch hold of the kitchen table to steady herself. Jane's alarm clock was on the table. Nine o'clock. It must have stopped. A lifetime ago it had been eight o'clock, and she and David had gone to bed. She was probably still in bed, dreaming that there was a fire. In a little while, she would wake up and tell him about it. "I dreamed that I had to save Shakespeare, and when I ran through the dining room, flames were bursting out from everywhere. . . ."

It was interesting to dream that you were dreaming. She could even hear the sound of the fire as it curled along the dining-room wall. She hadn't realized that fire made a noise, a hollow, crackling noise like bones breaking in a human body. It had probably frightened Shakespeare off the wing chair, because he was no longer there. She had to crawl under the sofa to find him, and he kept pulling his paw away just as she tried to catch hold of him. He'd always done that, even as a baby. . . . Baby. . . . A bell rang in her mind. There were lots of bells, all at once, and the dream became silly, as dreams usually did. The room was full of people now, all appearing out of nowhere. There was the tall plumber, and the short tailor, and the fat butcher and the electric-meter man, and everyone of them was dressed up like children in large fireman hats, and rubber coats that were too big for them.

"Hey there!" yelled the tall plumber. "What are you doing in here!"

"I'm looking for a yellow cat," said Claudia politely. . . .

She opened her eyes and saw Nancy Riddle, of all people. She wanted to ask her where on earth she'd come from, but she didn't have a great deal of breath, and it was more important to know about David and the children. She tried to sit up, but Nancy's restraining hand kept her down. "The children," said Nancy, "are fine. I sent them to my house with my chauffeur. You'll see them in the morning."

"But, Nancy, I have to get to David! The house is on fire!"

"You don't say," said Nancy. She held a flask to Claudia's lips. "Here. Drink this."

Claudia pushed it away. "I never drink, thanks."

"Well you'll drink now, thanks," said Nancy.

Claudia drank, surprised that Nancy had such a compelling way about her, in spite of her double chin and dry, gold hair. "Lucky for you," she went on severely, "that David's over at the barn and doesn't know you were scrabbling under the sofa in the middle of a fire looking for a cat. You ought to have your tail kicked. I thought you were supposed to be having another baby or something."

"I don't think the baby really minded," said

Claudia. "It's used to running around with me." The drink was getting warm inside of her. Although she hated the taste of whiskey, she found that once it got past her throat it wasn't so bad. It seemed to make her knees feel less like rubber, and to give her quite a lift in spirits. "This looks like a station wagon we're in," she discovered in mild astonishment.

"No looks about it. It is," said Nancy.

"Whose?"

"I don't know. Somebody's out there."

Claudia followed the vague direction of Nancy's bejeweled hand. Apparently a lot had been going on that she didn't know anything about. People and cars crowded the side lawn like a picnic, and in the bright glare of the many headlights, she could see the plumber in his fireman's hat, unfurling hose from an engine. A sublime sense of relaxation stole over her. Her house was burning down, but it had ceased to be a personal responsibility; it had become a community event. She sat up and watched the proceedings with a complete detachment. "How do they manage to carry all that water in those hoses?" she marveled.

Nancy stared at her.

Claudia repeated the question.

"I don't think you're overly bright," said Nancy.

"Oh, I'm not," Claudia conceded affably. "I never was. How do they?"

"You know perfectly well that they're pumping it from the brook."

"That's awfully smart of them," said Claudia.

Nancy leaned over Claudia's shoulder to peer out of the window. "They're doing a grand job for volunteers," she acknowledged respectfully. "You won't come off too badly. You'll have to rebuild a couple of rooms, but your insurance'll pay for it."

Insurance. The warm feeling that had been spreading through Claudia's veins abruptly vanished. Her blood froze. Like an idiot, she'd put her foot down on squandering hundreds of dollars every year against a fire that she was sure they'd never have. "It's quixotic to support insurance companies," she'd pointed out to David, and he had answered meekly, "Yes, Mama."

Now they had had the fire and David would never forgive her. "We haven't any insurance," she told Nancy weakly. "I made David give it up. I thought it was silly."

"My God," said Nancy.

"Could I please have another little drink?"

Nancy uncorked the silver flask. "For a girl who doesn't indulge," she remarked dryly, "you're doing all right."

By the time David sought them out, Claudia was again feeling very relaxed, and her spirits were even higher than before. "Isn't it wonderful," she greeted him, "that we only lost the dining room and nursery, and that nobody's hurt, and I think it was darling of the firemen to save the damned old sideboard."

David eyed her with a lift of his brows. "You'd better go home with Nancy," he advised, "and get a good night's sleep."

"I won't unless you will."

"I can't. I have to be here first thing in the morning to make a settlement with the insurance people."

"What do you mean insurance people?" she demanded.

"Just what I say."

"Claudia told me you didn't have any," Nancy put in.

"How many kinds of a jackass do you think I am?" said David.

Claudia's lips set into a grim line. "I must say," she mentioned coldly, "that I love the way you take your wife's advice."

It seemed strange to find their bedroom exactly as they had left it less than three hours before—except that Shakespeare had humped himself to sleep beneath the blankets. "The nerve!" cried Claudia. "Scat!"

With one accord they climbed into his place, and drew the covers to their tired chins. "Oh, Lord," breathed David, "this is good."

"I smell smoke," said Claudia.

"Go ahead and smell it," said David and put out the light.

"You know," said Claudia thoughtfully, "whisky's pretty good."

David sighed. "Are you going to get full of conversation again?"

"I think so," said Claudia. "Nancy was nice to take the children, wasn't she? I hope Matthew remembers he's housebroken."

"I hope so too," said David. He was silent for a moment, and then he added, as if to take back all the unkind things he had ever said about her, "She's a good old slob."

"Everybody's a good old slob," said Claudia with a little too much emotion. "Why should all those men tonight have run the risk of being burned to death to save somebody's house they hardly know?"

"That," said David, "is something a woman would never understand." He leaned over and kissed her.

"Your hair's the image of a singed chicken," she said drowsily. "And I do understand it if anyone should happen to drive up and ask you."

They were almost asleep when Edward and Jane came home from the movies. Claudia giggled as she heard their agitated footsteps, running through the living room.

"I must say I admire your peculiar brand of humor," said David sourly.

"I can't help it, they sound like mice on the roof upside down—" She broke off as a shrill scream tore the air. "That's Jane," she gasped, with mirth closing her windpipes, "she's got to the dining room!"

David suffered a sharp though delayed impact. He

began to laugh. They were both shaking with laughter by the time Jane and Edward reached the bedroom door. Edward plunged the room into a blaze of light without so much as knocking. Jane looked even funnier than she sounded, as she stood there blinking in the glare. Her mouth hung open, with lips like blobs of jelly over which she had no control. She tried to ask about the children, but the words came forth without shape or meaning.

Claudia took pity on her. "The children are fine," she said.

Edward took out his handkerchief and mopped his white face. "How did it start?" he asked thickly.

David was about to explain something about a defective cable, but Claudia nudged him to silence. "How did what start?" she asked crisply. "We've been asleep, we didn't know anything was wrong."

Edward swallowed his Adam's apple twice, but Jane, following through on her own tragic thoughts, began to sob with relief. "They could have all been burned to death," she wept, "and us not here to help them!"

Claudia sighed. "Jane's been drinking again," she murmured sadly.

Six

THERE WAS NOTHING EXCITING OR CHALLENGING about a fire that was out. It was just a plain messy business, full of ashes that had to be carted away, and the sporadic missing of something or other that had been burned up. Even the warm mellow feeling that Claudia had had for the plumber and the carpenter and the electrician faded into the more normal irritation of not being able to pin them down to building a new wing on the house. They were getting ready for the fishing season.

From a practical point of view she could not help thinking that it was unwise to replace what they had lost. There was no telling when David's commission would come through, and she and the children could make-shift without a dining room and the extra bedroom. But David didn't feel that way about it. He said, "Now look, we're fighting for a way of life." She knew what he meant, and he was right. Homes were being bombed, and people knew fear and hurt, but after a time they found the courage and the will to reconstruct what had been destroyed. "We'll build a new wing," said David, "that will make the old one look like two cents."

Ordinarily it was fun to plan even a shed or a chicken house. But now there was only anguish in the thought that he would probably be gone before the building was completed. It was the same with everything. It was hard to look forward to having a baby that he would not see. It was hard to face the pale glory of spring, knowing that he would not be with her to share the autumn. I can manage to be noble in spots, she thought, but I don't seem to be able to stay that way for long at a time.

In her more exalted moments, however, she pretended to be thrilled over the glass panels he was designing for the nursery. She even pretended to be thrilled when he filled the kitchen full of complicated electrical equipment, although her heart sank, and so did Jane's. "It's the only intelligent way to function," he pointed out to them. "It'll save you time and labor." They agreed that it would, but behind his back they washed the dishes by hand and loved it.

It was a new experience to live so fully each day that if there were never to be another day, one would have had a fill of happiness. It was a new experience to look at someone you loved as if it were the last time you would ever see him. David was doing the same thing. He didn't say so, but she could tell it by the way he kissed her, and the way he played with the dogs, and spoke to Bobby and Matthew. Nothing soft or tender—merely an awareness of being, that made each moment so sharply rich that sometimes she felt as if they had discovered the one great secret of living. It must be sad to die, she thought, and know that one had not loved enough, or suffered enough, or felt enough. Each morning that she kissed David good-bye, each evening that she met him at the station, was like a special grant from heaven, a beneficent tangle in the slow unwinding of red tape that continued to hold up his commission. But it was ready to go through, and almost any day he might come home and tell her that he had received his rank and destination. Each night she prayed, "Oh God, when it does happen, don't let him be sent to Africa, or Egypt or China—" There was Alaska, and Australia and Ireland too, but she knew that God got the general gist of the petition.

In the meantime, David worked like mad to get the farm in running order. The place needed a cash crop to help keep it going, and now Edward was selling eighty quarts of milk and ten dozen eggs a day, in addition to a less regular source of income from the sale of young stock. Julia and Hartley thought that David was out of his head. Julia talked to Claudia about it in private. "Why don't you make him give up the farm? Edward might break a leg, and then where are you? Cows to milk, pipes to freeze, fuses to blow."

"Jane and I aren't imbeciles; we could take over in

an emergency," Claudia replied. But down deep within her, she agreed with Julia—it would be far less responsibility and expense to move into an apartment. Yet she hated to suggest it, for David had a strange conviction that if he left her on the farm he was leaving her in tender hands. Besides, he said that the war would not last forever, and if people gave up the fundamentals of life, there would be nothing to come back to. "Unless you'd rather?" he asked her searchingly. "Tell me, truthfully. Would you be happier if we sold the place? We can, you know. Small productive farms are at a premium, now."

"I'd be terribly unhappy if we sold it," she told him, because she knew it was the answer that he wanted to hear. "And I think," she went on, "that I'd better learn to run the tractor."

"Running a tractor," said David, "is just what the well-dressed lady in her seventh month should be doing." He compromised, though, and taught her how to run the milking machine. He taught her, too, why it was necessary to rotate crops and replenish the earth. "You can't keep taking off, you have to put back," he said. For the first time she began to realize how the stock and the land were one. She began to know the great and deep satisfaction of looking forward to a field of emerald green alfalfa. She began to worry whether it would be a good hay year, and would they get enough corn to fill the silo.

She took hold for his sake, but it wasn't long before she found herself interested for her own sake. It was work to do, and she did it. Sometimes, though, she felt that she wasn't doing anything at all, because it was so simple to do the thing at hand. She envied other women who were really active in the war. Elizabeth was learning to be a welder, of all things, and Nancy was taking poison gas and bombs in New York three times a week, and Julia was the head of something with a lot of initials, and spent most of her time in Washington. "I'm a total loss," Claudia complained to David.

"For a total loss," said David, looking at her in a very special way, "you're doing quite a lot for your country." He worried that she was doing a little too much and so did Jane. "Mr. Naughton, I think it's my duty to tell you I found Mrs. Naughton up on the stepladder fussing with the new curtains," she reported to him one evening.

"Sneak!" Claudia hissed.

"Jane's perfectly right," said David. "Please remember half that baby's mine.—When's the last time you went into town to the doctor?"

"I'm supposed to go this week," she admitted.

"Make it tomorrow," he said, "and you can meet me for the final fitting of my uniform."

Her heart dragged to a leaden stop within her. It

was his way of telling her that the red tape was unwinding to an end.

She washed her hair before she went to bed because her nails were a mess from planting. She tried on her tweed suit, too.

"How do I look?" she demanded.

"Nice," said David. "Your hair always looks nice after it's washed."

"My hair. Why should I care what my hair looks like?"

"Oh," he said. "Turn around."

She turned around. "Could you tell?"

"Tell what?"

"Please be serious. . . . Don't you think I'm remarkable?"

He pulled her to him. "Very remarkable," he said huskily.

Bobby came in. "You're always kissing," he said in disgust.

"Don't you like it?" David queried.

"No," said Bobby. "It's sissy."

"That," said David, "is where you're wrong." He made a face. "You smell."

"I ate an onion."

"Yes, I forgot to tell you," said Claudia. "He's got a crush on onions."

"Jane says it's good for the blood," Bobby defended.

"What blood?" asked David.

Bobby looked harassed. He addressed himself to his mother, and changed the subject. "Where are you going?"

"No place. But you're going to bed, Mister. Come on. Kiss. Goodnight."

He presented his cheek by the infinitesimal extension of his neck muscles.

"Don't hurt yourself." She caught him by the nose and kissed him roundly.

"Quit it!" said Bobby, full of manhood. "Why are you dressed up to go out?" he reverted.

"So Daddy won't have to wait around for me in the morning." She cleared her throat nonchalantly. "Do you notice anything?"

Bobby observed her critically. "You have on a new suit."

"New shape," David corrected sotto voce.

Jane put in an irate appearance. "So that's where you disappeared to, young man." She set her lips. "He was reading again where he shouldn't ought to."

"Bobby, that's a bad habit," said David gravely. "You'll regret it when you grow up."

"Look who's talking," Claudia said.

Jane blushed. Children under ten were different. She changed the subject. "That suit could do with a pressing, Mrs. Naughton."

"I'd love it if you would," said Claudia gratefully. "How do you think I look?"

Jane's blush grew hotter. Her attitude toward sex remained consistent to the bitter end, and she was of the opinion that babies should be heard but not seen. "You look tired," she evaded. "I'll fix you a cup of hot tea after you're in bed."

"You do that," said David. "And when I'm not here, you keep on being the policeman of the family, Jane."

Bobby pricked up his ears. "When are you going, Dad?" he asked eagerly.

"You know as much about it as I do."

"Come along, Bobby," said Jane quickly. She couldn't bear the war. She couldn't bear to think of David leaving. Claudia suddenly couldn't bear it either. She hurried into the closet to take off her suit. "Oh God, please, please . . ." she whispered.

She caught the one-thirty express from Bridgeport the following day. It was a much longer drive than to the local Eastbrook depot, but Edward had to go there anyway to pick up some parts for the manure spreader. "I might as well save gas and tires and take the children for shoes," said Jane, so they all piled in the station wagon, and looked like immigrants. At the last minute, Bluff and Bluster jumped in too, and at once the car took on an air of decayed gentry. There's nothing, thought Claudia, like a brace of Great Danes to elevate one's social aura.

"Phew," Jane suddenly discovered.

"You'll get used to it," said Claudia.

Shakespeare appeared from his usual vicinity of nowhere, and executed a busy schottische in pursuit of a leaf. His amber eyes, however, were full of sour grapes. "Take him along," Matthew ordered imperiously.

Jane would have cheerfully cut off her right hand at Matthew's behest, but she drew the line at shopping with a cat. "Mind your feet on Jane's nice clean skirt," said she.

Matthew did not mind his feet. Bobby, who had recently appointed himself the custodian of Matthew's morals and behavior, took exception to his disobedience. "Do as Jane tells you," he ordered. "You're a spoiled brat."

"He's no such thing!" cried Jane with a most peculiar shift of attitude.

"He is too," insisted Bobby. "I heard Daddy say so."

"I'm not!" Matthew bellowed, transferring his footwiping to Bobby's shins.

Bobby's wrath exploded. "I'm going to kill you if you don't watch out!" he threatened.

Jane clicked her tongue. "That's not nice," said Edward mildly. "I'm surprised at such talk," Claudia followed up, with no great degree of concern. They were growing up fast, she mused, and from now on the house would probably be full of constant noise and fighting. It would be rather wonderful to have a little girl for a change. Not quite as tempestuous, perhaps, but comforting, and somehow ladylike. She thought, as she saw all the heads bobbing behind her, This is the way it's going to be without David. There was a dull, heavy ache all over her body, and in her heart and soul. She could smile and talk and even laugh above it, but it was always there. It was the ache of war, and a woman had to learn to live with it, and rise above it, or else not live at all.

"What kind of emblem is Dad going to have on his uniform?" Bobby suddenly inquired. He, too, was always thinking of the war, but he was pleased and excited about it, for he had not yet tasted the emptiness of a household without a father. "Is it going to be a silver bar?"

"That's only a second lieutenant," said Edward.

Bobby hooted at his ignorance. "No it isn't, a second lieutenant's a gold bar!"

"And a captain," Claudia intoned softly, "is two silver bars, and a major is a gold oak leaf." Strange new lessons she was learning these days. Six months ago she would not have known the distinction between a private and a general. Now she noticed every uniform she saw. Six months ago, Tobruk, Darwin and Chungking had been remote geography. Now they were a part of her own front yard.

David was amazed at her sudden mastery of the maps. She knew exactly where everything was in the line of oceans and continents and even islands. "I didn't know you had it in you," he complimented her.

"It's not really bona fide," she confessed. "I mean it's not the sort of inborn intelligence that Julia has, or women who opinionate over the radio, and run for things. It's just that I want to be prepared ahead of time for all the places where you might be sent."

"And you admit it."

"Certainly I admit it."

"But what's one life?"

"One life is all lives," she said.

"You might have something there," he answered soberly.

She realized suddenly that they had reached the station square, and Jane was talking to her. "Whilst we're here in Bridgeport, how about having Matthew's hair cut?"

"Oh, dear," said Claudia. "I hate to." If Matthew's golden curls were shaven off, his ears would come out and he'd be irrevocably grown-up. David would like that, though, and it might make him feel easier about going away. "Off with his hair," she misquoted briskly, from her only stand-by. "One baby in the house will be enough."

Jane quickly knocked on wood. "As long as you're in the seventh month now, you could sort of look around and see what the shops have in the way of perambulators," she suggested.

"I think," said Claudia, as she also knocked on wood, "we'll get a perambulator from Aunt Julia for a present. But I'll look around anyway, just in case."

"Don't, if you're tired. Be sure you don't get tired," Jane warned her.

Claudia scoffed at fatigue. "I'm a horse," she said. "I'm never tired."

It was odd that she should have been tired by the time she reached New York. She couldn't imagine why—sitting still in a train—and yet she was tired. It was probably because she didn't have anything to do, but think. It was probably because she kept trying to read the newspaper of the man who shared her seat. It was always a strain to do that, particularly when the owner of the newspaper seemed to go out of his way to make it difficult. The news, however, was important. Trouble was starting in the Coral Sea, and another great convoy of American troops had landed in Northern Ireland. The war surrounded the world. There was no part of the globe that was free of peril and bloodshed.

It was hot and sultry in New York. No sooner did she step out on Forty-second Street than she had the horrid feeling of two feet in one shoe. The Fifth Avenue bus seemed far away. She hailed a taxi.

It wasn't a very long drive uptown. She held a fifty-cent piece in readiness and bet with herself that it would be just right, including tip. It was. The taxi rounded the corner, and drew to a stop before Dr.

Rowland's office, with the meter registering a neat forty cents. Then click—it dropped an extra nickel. "That's plain nasty," she muttered, digging into her purse to make up the additional five cents. She could only find three cents and a quarter. Her soul writhed in conflict. David always said that women were congenital dime-tippers. Well, she would show him that it wasn't true. She took a deep breath, gave the driver the whole quarter, and told him to keep the change.

He almost fell over, which bore out David's contention. The incident seemed to change his opinion of the entire female sex; he couldn't do enough for her. He practically lifted her out of the cab, and with her elbow firmly cradled in the palm of his hand, he gently guided her across the sidewalk.

It was a little too much of a good thing, for she liked to walk by herself and open doors by herself, and get in and out of places by herself. Too much etiquette got on her nerves, and she was thankful that David was the sort of man who was born courteous, and didn't have to bother with politeness. Simply as a matter of routine, he insisted on Bobby rising at the table when she sat down or got up, which was sufficient manners for the whole family.

The taxi driver, however, exceeded anything she had ever before experienced in the line of chivalry. She might have been some sort of valuable egg the way he escorted her up the stoop. "You got to be careful," he mentioned largely.

I wonder, thought Claudia, stiffening, if he means anything by that.

"I got a couple of my own," he continued, laying his cards on the table.

Inasmuch as she was hard on the way to topping his record, it was hard to resist a little bragging on her own account, although to do so would have acknowledged his association of ideas. True, Dr. Rowland's elegant brass name plate was right in front of them, but there was no reason why he couldn't have been a nose-and-throat man.

"Yes, sir," the taxi driver went on in genial camaraderie. "Both boys, and both in the Army."

Claudia at once lost all pique. Anybody who had anybody in the Army was a kind of blood relation as far as she was concerned. "I have a husband in the Army too," she offered eagerly.

He gave a low whistle of sympathy. "With a baby coming, that's pretty tough," he said.

"Oh, I have two other children," she hastened to explain, with no desire to brag at this point, but merely to clarify that she was an old hand at the business. "My husband felt he ought to go," she added with a small but very definite swagger creeping in.

The taxi driver gave her swagger for swagger. "My boys didn't wait to be drafted, either, they enlisted, too. One's eighteen, the other's twenty. Abe—that's the oldest one, he's in coast artillery—he's in Australia. I don't know where Morty is. I have a feeling it's Iceland. But I'm not telling the missus."

Claudia's heart ached for the missus. "How does she feel about it?" she asked.

"She feels terrible," said the taxi driver, simply. "I say to her, 'Sarah, you ain't the only one.' She says she knows she ain't the only one."

"I don't think that helps very much," said Claudia. "It's a personal war just the same."

"I guess it is," he agreed. "If you haven't got anybody in it, it's easy enough to look at it big. Sure. I know how Sarah feels. I talk to her about freedom and liberty and all she talks back to me is Abe and Morty."

"Don't scold her for it," said Claudia.

"I don't scold her," he said. "I just say to her, 'What can we do about it, Sarah? We got to take it.'" He dug into his pocket and drew out a new leatherette folder with two pictures in it. "That's them," he said. "The one that's smiling is Morty."

"They're both smiling," said Claudia.

"The one that's smiling most," he amended.

"They're handsome," said Claudia, thinking mainly of their souls. They'd very likely been beautiful when they were little. She was about to take out the snapshot of Matthew and Bobby that she carried in her purse, when Miss Kennedy opened the door and ushered out a patient—a very fat lady who probably wasn't fat at all.

"Well," said Claudia, "I have to go now." She held

out her hand to the taxi driver. "Good-bye," she said.
"When you write to Abe and Morty, wish them luck
for me. And give Sarah my love."

"I will," he promised, walking backwards down
the steps. "And the same to you and your husband."

Miss Kennedy clapped her hand over her mouth.
"I thought he was your taxi driver!" she tittered.
"Isn't that a scream?"

"It certainly is," said Claudia. She waved to him as
he got into his cab. He waved back, and drove away.

Dr. Rowland took her blood pressure, and talked
about the war. He said he couldn't get any decent
office nurse, they were all going into service, and how
was help on the farm?

"Fine," said Claudia.

"You're lucky," he said. He looked at her card and
jotted down her blood pressure. "How do you feel
in general?"

"Fine," she said.

"That's fine," he nodded. "Come in again in two
weeks."

If I had known he wasn't going to examine me, I
wouldn't have wasted my best underwear, she
thought, disgruntled. It was just as well, however, not
to have to go through all the usual rigmarole, because
now she'd have time to look at perambulators before
she met David.

She not only looked at perambulators, she began

to buy the layette. It was wonderful to start from scratch. With Matthew inheriting everything from Bobby, there wasn't a thing left, not even a didie.

The salesgirl thought it was her first baby. Claudia didn't bother to disillusion her. "It'll be my first girl, anyway," she told herself.

Before she knew it, it was half past four. For an hour, she had forgotten the war, forgotten that she was to meet David to try on his uniform. It was like coming back from a dream into a nightmare.

"Are you tired, madam?" the salesgirl asked solicitously.

"A little," Claudia admitted, and let it go at that. She wondered what people's hearts would look like these days, if their smiles were suddenly stripped away.

She was more than ever conscious of the determined curve of her lips as she sat in a chair watching David try on his uniform. He was like a bride with her wedding gown, or better yet, he was like one of their drakes preening up his feathers. Fortunately, he was too worried about his left shoulder to notice the untruthfulness of her smile. "It's not quite right," he frowned.

"I'd leave it alone, sir," the tailor advised. "I wouldn't touch it. I think it's perfect."

"Claudia, what do you think?"

"I think it's perfect, too," said Claudia. "It's wrong for any one man to be so handsome."

He turned back to the mirror. She thought, Now I know where Bobby gets that little self-conscious grin from. There was something heartbreaking about it, something about it that made her want to put her arms around him. But she had a sense that he would not know that her arms held him. The war had already given him wings.

"Where shall I send it, sir?"

"I might as well take it," said David nonchalantly.

"Why drag it around?" Claudia asked.

He looked disappointed. "As long as it fits, I might as well have it."

"But you can't wear it yet," she pointed out in pitiful triumph. "Not till you've gotten your commission."

"I know that." He looked sheepish. "I could try it on for Bobby tonight, though."

She thought, What a beast I am to spoil his pleasure. "Of course, take it," she said. "It would be silly not to."

It was a flat enough package, but it was sizable and heavy, and kept getting in the way as they went down in the crowded elevator. It's like another person with us, Claudia thought.

There was a half an hour to kill before train time, so they went to David's office. "I'd like to pick up a set of blueprints," he said.

"Why don't you be honest? You want to show off your uniform to Roger."

"Unpack this box? I'm not crazy."

"You wouldn't need a second invitation."

"You don't love me," he accused her. "Otherwise you'd talk kindly to me."

"I talk very kindly to you," she said.

Their gayety was forced. It was as if she were a little ashamed because she wasn't happy, and David was a little ashamed because he was.

Roger was busy with a client as they passed his door. He called out to David, "Look on your desk!" There was a note in his voice that made Claudia know at once. She knew, even before David knew. It came as a complete surprise to him. "Well, I'll be damned," he said slowly, as he picked up the yellow telegram.

"It's come," Claudia's lips moved, but the words carried no sound with them. She thought, I'd better sit down.

"Well, I'll be damned," said David again. A slow grin spread over his face. "CAPTAIN DAVID NAUGHTON," he read aloud. "They've made me a captain!"

"Dear God," Claudia swiftly prayed, "help me to take it decently. Even if it's China. Amen."

"Open it!" she whispered.

"Look," he reminded her robustly. "No matter where I'm going, I'm coming back, you know."

"Yes, I know. I'm just anxious to be rid of you."

"That's a fine way to talk to a captain."

"I knew they'd make you a captain! Next you'll be a colonel—"

"No major in your man's army?"

She shook her head. "Next step a colonel," she insisted, "and then a commander."

"Hey," he stopped her, "you're in the Navy."

She wondered why he wasn't opening the telegram. He just stood there, trying to make conversation, putting off the moment. All of a sudden, he's scared too, she realized.

"Open it, darling," she said again. Her voice was steady. It was strange how his weakness could make her strong.

The ticking of the clock on his desk filled the room as he tore the envelope, and unfolded the yellow slip of paper. He read it. She saw his eyes widen. He held it closer, and read it again.

"What is it?" her lips moved, but once more her voice was gone.

Silently, he gave her the telegram. The paper shook in her hands. "Goose!" he said harshly. "Read it!"

She wet her lips. "Where is Bridgeport?"

"Bridgeport," said he, "is in its usual place."

"But there must be a lot of Bridgeports—Bridgeport, Australia? Bridgeport, England?" Her courage faltered. "Maybe Bridgeport, Egypt?"

"As far as I know," said David shortly, "there's only one Bridgeport. And that's Bridgeport, Connecticut."

"But that's our Bridgeport!" she gasped. "It can't be!"

"Why not? It's a defense town, and you can't have defense workers without buildings and you can't have buildings without architects."

She stared at him. "Please don't fool me," she besought him.

"I'm not fooling you," he said. "It's there in black and white."

Her sanity gave way. His arms were around her. They were strong and tight and kept her from shaking to pieces. "Darling, what's wrong?" he exclaimed in alarm.

If he was so stupid that he didn't know why she was crying, she couldn't stop to tell him. "It—it's only nineteen m-miles away—you can come home every night—" she sobbed.

"But that's nothing to cry about!" he protested.

"You're not supposed to cry," she gulped, "when you've got something to cry about—it's only when you haven't—"

"You poor old monkey-face," he said, with a kind of awe. He seemed to understand for the first time the way women felt. He drew her closer to him, and she felt his lips pressed hard against her hair.

She was aware of Roger tiptoeing into the room. She had no shame. Ordinarily she would rather have died than let anyone see her cry, but this was different.

Roger's face screwed up with pity. "He'll come back," he tried to comfort her.

"He can't come back!" sobbed Claudia, "because he isn't going away!"

By the time she stopped crying, they had missed the train. "I'll have to phone Jane we won't be there for supper," she said. "But it doesn't matter, it's only meat balls."

"I don't feel like meat balls tonight," said David. "Let's go out and celebrate. Dinner, theatre—we'll even stay in town to sleep!"

"At Julia and Hartley's?" she queried doubtfully. "I'd feel more at home at home."

"Certainly not. This is no family affair. We'll go to a hotel."

She took fire at once. "Put on your uniform, and I'll be a war bride!"

David's eyebrow climbed his forehead. "Don't be so technical," she forestalled him impatiently.

She telephoned Jane while he undressed in Roger's office. Jane was disappointed about the meat balls because she had switched to liver in Bridgeport. "It looked so nice and fresh," she explained. "And also, Matthew got his haircut."

"Oh, yes," said Claudia. "I forgot. His haircut. Is he very homely?"

"He's not homely at all," cried Jane indignantly. "He just looks different. . . . How did Mr. Naughton look in his uniform?"

"Captain Naughton," Claudia corrected, "looks out-and-out handsome."

Jane had grown to be quite quick in catching on to things. "His commission came through!" she quavered. She lost courage. "I guess he'll be going away now," she finished lamely.

"Yes," said Claudia, enjoying cruelty to the utmost. "And it's not China. Nor yet again Alaska."

"You're a dirty devil!" David called out to her.

"Captain Naughton says I'm a dirty devil," she relayed to Jane, "so I won't tease you. It's Bridgeport."

Bridgeport didn't mean a thing to Jane. She said she'd never heard of it, and it took a full minute for her to comprehend that it was the Bridgeport where Matthew just had his hair cut. When she finally did begin to realize it, she got all choked up and couldn't speak, which was sheer waste of a long-distance call. "You'd better let me talk to Bobby," said Claudia thriftily.

"Jane wasn't as noisy as I was," she told David later, "but I could tell that she was crying."

"I give up," said David, looking baffled.

"Don't be silly," said Claudia. "I'd have been disappointed if she hadn't cried."

"What did Bobby say?"

"Bobby said 'Whoopeee!' when he heard that you'd been made a Captain."

"What did he say about Bridgeport?"

Claudia hesitated. Bobby's reaction to Bridgeport

had been somewhat of a shock to her. Having expected Australia at the very nearest, he regarded Bridgeport as a distinct anticlimax. "He seemed to think," she admitted reluctantly, "that it wasn't very exciting."

"It's not," said David tersely.

She was swift to sense the bitter disappointment in his answer. "I think you really want to go away and leave me," she accused him half in jest.

"You know that's not true."

She didn't say anything for a moment. She knew that she ought not to press him, for he would not want to hurt her, nor would he lie to her. A part of him wanted to stay with her and the children, but another part of him demanded the adventure and the challenge of going forth to meet the enemy. She felt as if she had betrayed him. She had begged God behind his back not to send him too far away, and God had answered her prayers. Indeed in His great and abundant generosity, He had literally tied David to her apron strings. She had never dreamed of his being stationed twenty miles away; she wouldn't have had the nerve to ask for it. But God had stepped down from His heaven, and with His own hand had picked the most perfect spot.

"Do you think it's because of the baby coming that God let you stay in Bridgeport?" she asked David, a little timidly at dinner.

She realized too late that it was the wrong approach. David wasn't on intimate speaking terms with God. He didn't even call God by His first name. He preferred to say, "Fate", or "Destiny", or even "Life". Now he shrugged. "Believe me," he said grimly, "God's not worrying His head about us."

"I'm pretty sure He's around, though," said Claudia.

"Why?" asked David flatly.

"Because," said Claudia, "if even one person in the world is as grateful and happy as I am, He must be some place, to have done it."

"I'd like to get my hands on a Jap," David muttered, irrelevantly. He picked up the menu. "What do you want to eat?"

"What do you want to eat, *darling?*" she corrected.

"Darling," he repeated obediently.

"I feel like a mistress," she sulked, "trying to win you away from your wife; your wife being the war. . . . What hotel do we go to?"

"First decide what you want to eat."

"A nice steak?" the waiter suggested.

"No steak," said Claudia. Two dollars and a half for one little steak was robbery. "That's without even coffee," she reminded David in an undertone.

"We'll have two steaks," said David. "Rare. And French fried potatoes, and a bowl of mixed green salad. . . . And one Camembert cheese, and chocolate ice cream for Madame."

"Pistachio," Claudia interrupted. "Be sure to rub the bowl with garlic. The salad bowl, I mean."

"And let me see your wine card," David added.

The bill was slowly mounting to a fortune, but wisdom told her to simply smile and bear it. There was a time to spend and a time to save, and tonight was the time to spend. He would probably take a suite at the most expensive hotel in town, and she wouldn't lift a finger to stop him. Either I'm a mouse or a mistress, she decided.

"I wish," she said aloud, "that I looked slim and stylish and beautiful enough to be with the handsomest officer in the restaurant."

"You look," said David, "like a little girl dressed up with a pillow." He caught her hand beneath the table. "I love you, darling."

Her eyes filled with tears because she understood him so well. "Maybe you won't have to stay in Bridgeport for the duration," she said. "Maybe you'll get a chance to go to China later—"

"Maybe," he agreed gently. "Thanks, anyway."

"You're welcome," she said. She felt that she could afford to be lavish with the future, for in all their life together she had never known such full and utter happiness. If they were to be bombed tomorrow, they would have had this night together.

The waiter placed two sizzling steaks before them. He poured the wine. The orchestra played. "This is Heaven," said Claudia. "Sheer Heaven." She felt sorry for all the people who weren't in Heaven with them. She also felt a little dizzy, and she had a funny pain somewhere deep inside of her. "I shouldn't have eaten when I was so excited," she thought.

The attendant in the rest room gave her an aspirin. When she returned to the table, David was asking for the check. He rose as she approached, and waited, standing, until she sat down, like an imitation of himself teaching Bobby manners. A warm glow went through her. "I think I shall insist on politeness from now on," she said. "I like it."

"That wasn't politeness," said David. "It was just a way of telling you you're all the woman I want."

"I can't understand why," she said humbly.

"I can't either. I'm just funny that way."

The waiter brought the check. She couldn't help seeing the amount, and it was enormous, as she knew it would be.

"How much should I give him?" David asked. He seemed loath to ruin a lovely evening by incurring her disfavor with his usual generosity when it came to tipping.

"Sixty cents is plenty," she said, with perfect logic. "A cleaning woman gets less than that an hour."

He looked miserable. "We had wine, remember."

"What on earth difference does that make? The bottle wasn't heavy to carry."

David was gentle but firm. "It's the principle. I can't give him less than a dollar."

She was secretly elated, for she couldn't have borne to be married to a stingy man. Just the same, she could never see the point of splashing quarters all over a plate for service that the restaurant should have paid for itself—although she'd have hated it if he hadn't. "Darling," she said exultantly, "give the waiter two dollars, one from me—with love."

David laughed, but he looked pleased as he laid two crisp bills across the plate.

"I tipped a taximan twenty-five cents today for a little tiny ride," she confessed shyly. "For the good of my soul."

"Splendid!" he applauded. "I bet your soul looks beautiful."

"It does," she said. "Wait'll you see."

The waiter sidled up to the table and whisked the plate away. "Thank you, sir!" he exclaimed. "Thank you very much!"

"He was surprised," said Claudia. "Maybe he has a son in the war. My taximan had two."

"Two what?"

"Two sons, of course. Abe and Morty. One's in Australia. Coast Artillery. The other he thinks is in Iceland, maybe. But he hasn't told Sarah. Sarah's his wife."

"What did you do, have lunch with the man?"

"No," said Claudia, "we just talked." Her voice brooded. "I thought of Sarah when I found out that you were going to stay in Bridgeport. Poor thing."

"It takes a bit of mental gymnastics to get the connection," said David.

"But you do."

"Yes," said David soberly, "I do."

Claudia sighed. "The world must be full of Sarahs."

"Don't think of them tonight," said David. "Just think of us.—Shall we go?"

She nodded. That funny pain was closing in on her again, but it would doubtless pass. She caught hold of the chair to steady herself.

"What's the matter?" asked David.

"Nothing." She tried to laugh. "The wine went to my head."

"We'd better not go to the theatre. I don't like the way you look."

She wanted to make a flippant and slightly bawdy retort, but the pain lashed out at her again. She was frightened. This was no ordinary pain. It was sharp and thick. It whipped across her back and struck at her inmost being as if to tear her into two. And then it was gone. She straightened up. "I'm all right now."

"No you're not," said David. "We're getting out of here."

She couldn't remember much of what happened after that. Agony crept up on her, and filled the world and blocked out thought and reason. The night became a montage of lights and hands and voices. David was there, only sometimes he was Dr. Rowland.

"Well, well, well, young lady. This is too bad."

"Don't worry, darling—everything's going to be all right. . . ."

One was fighting with her, the other was fighting for her. It was like the war. She tried to remember what the war was about. It was about life. This was life. A baby was coming into the world. . . . It was her baby. It was David's baby. . . . She must fight . . . fight . . . fight. . . .

They gave her merciful oblivion.

A thin cry sounded. It went away again, but it had sounded. She had heard her baby's salute to life, and so she slept. When she opened her eyes, David was bending over her. "Darling—" he whispered. "Thank God you're safe."

"I want to see the baby—"

"Later."

"Is it all right?"

"Yes."

"It's a little girl."

"Don't talk, darling."

"I knew it would be a little girl. Is it weak, David?"

"No dear."

"Seventh month babies sometimes are—"

"Yes, darling, they sometimes are."

He put his cheek against hers. It was his way of telling her. She did not have to ask. The baby had not lived.

"Thank God you're safe—" he whispered again. "Thank God I'm not in China, thank God I can be with you."

He wasn't talking to her, he was talking to God. That was strange—David talking to God. God had turned His face to David, and had left her in darkness. He had chosen to fill her with richness, and then He had caused her to be empty. She had never known such emptiness could be. David would not understand, because he had never borne a child. She knew that she must go through this alone—alone with all the other women in the world who were knowing emptiness and loss. She thought, There isn't any God. But she saw the humble gratitude in David's face, and she knew that if even one person in the world could look like that, then God was somewhere, like the sun.

Seven

BECAUSE IT WAS A THOUGHT CREATED OUT OF GRIEF, and purified with suffering, it did not stay with her. She remembered thinking it, she remembered thinking that if God were somewhere like the sun, she would have to wait for night to pass. But the darkness did not lift. She was aware that morning came, yet it was as if she were caught in a tunnel and could not see the light. She knew that the light was there, and that life was going on as always, but the tunnel had no ending.

No one knew that she was in the tunnel. That was the strange and terrifying part of it. "You've come through this very nicely," Dr. Rowland approved, and promptly washed his hands of her, except to poke his head in at the door when he was making rounds. The house physician poked his head in too, and the superintendent of nurses stopped by for a chat whenever she could. Claudia felt like an old habitué of the hospital, for she had been on the same floor three times—twice for babies, and once for appendicitis. The operation had been fun as soon as the gas pains stopped, but the babies had been fun from start to finish. At least they seemed so in retrospect, for time had softened the experiences into pleasant interludes involving very little labor, and two bouncing specimens of future citizens.

Now, however, it was all very different. Julia took time off from the war and came to see her on the third day with a box of new nightgowns. "I thought you'd need these."

"Thanks. I do. I haven't a thing—it happened so unexpectedly." She could have kicked her voice for trembling, but Julia didn't notice. "It's too bad," she said, "but frankly a miscarriage isn't the worst thing, with the world as it is. I don't mean," she amended hastily, "that one should go out and ask for it, but since it's happened, it's probably for the best."

"It wasn't a miscarriage," Claudia said. "The baby lived for an hour. It was a little girl. I heard it cry."

"Well anyway," Julia continued, "it isn't as if you'd had a chance to grow fond of it."

Claudia made no reply. Julia wasn't heartless, it was merely that she had never had any children, so they couldn't even talk about it together. She was glad when Julia left. She lay with her face to the wall and let the tears come. Outside in the corridor, nurses were carrying the babies to their mothers. Every three hours she would hear them go back and forth. She could visualize what was going on in the room next door, the room down the hall.

The door opened. Miss Carey rustled in. She was

a good nurse, with spectacles, and it was a shame to waste her with nothing to do. Miss Carey probably felt the same way. There was no little bundle to lay at Claudia's side, no delicate new contact over which to officiate. Time hung heavy on her capable hands.

Harried with a sense of having let her down, Claudia searched her immediate wants. "May I have a glass of water?" she asked.

"No, sir," said Miss Carey emphatically. "That would be bringing coals to Newcastle."

"Newcastle hurts."

"I know. Another couple of days, you won't have to be bound so tightly."

Claudia bit her lips. Her breasts were a constant reproach, with the excruciating pain of life, dammed back. She girded herself to ask the question that stuck in her throat whenever she tried to put it into words. "Did the baby open its eyes?"

"Now what kind of talk is that!" Miss Carey evaded crisply. "You'll have another one before you know it."

I'd be afraid to have another child, thought Claudia, suddenly. Afraid that I mightn't be able to carry it through. It was strange how fear could come to one. One had to go through a thing in order to gain significance. She supposed it was the same with everything. She had never given a thought to automobile accidents until David had been almost killed in one. She'd never been afraid of fire, until their house burned. She'd never realized the dangers of pregnancy—until now. She shuddered as she remembered how she had climbed fences, and stood on stepladders. She was obsessed by the thought that she had brought this grief upon herself. Dr. Rowland had told her it wasn't so, and David told her the same thing. But it had happened and she could only feel bewilderment and rebellion, and an overwhelming inadequacy. She had failed David, and the new soul that their love had summoned into being.

"If there's nothing I can do for you," Miss Carey broke in upon her thoughts, "I'll be outside. Ring if you want me."

"I will," said Claudia, knowing that there would be no need to ring.

When Dr. Rowland put in his fleeting appearance a little later, she stopped him firmly. "I don't need a special nurse," she said.

Dr. Rowland walked over to the bureau, plucked a carnation from a vase and stuck it in his lapel while he studied her chart. "Very well," he agreed. "I'll be glad to have Miss Carey for another case. We're short of nurses."

"She's yours," said Claudia.

Miss Carey entertained no hard feelings about being dismissed. She went off duty that same evening. "Good-bye," she said brusquely. "Better luck next time."

"Thank you," said Claudia.

After a time she rang for the floor nurse. She didn't want David to see her with reddened eyes.

The floor nurse was a probationer, with a round unfurnished face that looked as if she hadn't moved into it. Part and parcel with her face, she had fat legs and a healthy behind that made her skirts go up in the air whenever she bent over. "Everybody calls me Polly," she said, as she gave Claudia a basin and a towel and some soap on the bed tray. "I guess you can manage this by yourself. I'll be right back." She was very busy, however, and didn't show up for almost an hour. Claudia thought about asking for another favor, but she didn't want to be left stranded with David due at any moment.

He came at last, opening the door stealthily, afraid she might have fallen asleep.

"Idiot," she said.

He sat down beside her and held her close. His handsomeness in uniform was still a little shock to her. "It's like being married to a man all your life," she told him, "and then suddenly having him shave his moustache off—"

"I never wore a moustache."

"Don't be silly," she said.

He observed her closely. "You look different too. What is it?"

"A nightgown, instead of a hospital sack. Julia brought it. Much more expensive than I'd buy for myself. Handmade. Look."

He looked. "Is that good?"

"It's supposed to be excellent."

He rubbed his cheek against hers. "Darling, how do you feel?"

"Fine. . . . Tell me about what happened today. Are you liking it?"

"It's fairly interesting. Too early to tell. Not very exciting as yet. Nevertheless, Bridgeport has its distinct advantages for the time being."

"Isn't it permanent?" she asked swiftly.

"As far as I know," he reassured her.

She knocked on wood. He changed the subject. "Are you uncomfortable?"

"Pretty. . . . Oh, and talking of that, you owe me seven dollars a day and meals."

"You're not worth it."

"I know it," she agreed bleakly. "I'm not worth anything."

"Hey, listen!" he protested. "None of this inferiority business."

"Anyway, I let Miss Carey go."

He frowned. "That wasn't smart."

"Dr. Rowland said it was all right. There's not a thing for her to do," she added with difficulty.

David drew her head to his shoulder. "Look here, I'm the gentleman you used to sleep with. You don't have to put on a show for me."

She cried, then. "I ought to be ashamed," she sobbed between the great waves of grief that shook her. "I have no right to make you go through this at the end of a hard day."

"You have no right not to," he said.

The hospital was still, and the corridors dark when he finally rose to leave her. She called him from the door. "David, I love you so," she whispered.

"I love you too," he whispered back. "More than ever."

She fell asleep, as if his love were holding her in invisible arms. She slept dreamlessly until the dawn. She wakened as the sweet, grinding whimper of a baby passed through the hall outside. Her breasts were full. The hours stretched ahead of her, dreary and empty.

Dr. Rowland said she ought to have plenty of company to distract her, and presto, the days were crowded with visitors. Hartley and Roger and Elizabeth Van Doren, and Edith Dexter—and one afternoon, of all people, Helen Drew. "What did you do," Claudia asked David suspiciously, "put an ad in the paper? 'Come and see my wife'?"

"Well, business certainly picked up," he boasted, waving toward the bureau with its burden of loot.

She wondered whether she ought to tell him that she would rather be alone, or whether she should try to fight off the unhappy effect that company was beginning to have upon her. Sometimes when there were people in the room, she was overcome by an inexplicable sense of panic. Her pulses would pound up into her temples, and her hands grow moist, and the smile upon her face freeze into a grimace. Fortunately, no one seemed to notice anything amiss, so it became merely a question of holding on to herself until she was alone again. Then she would lie with her eyes closed and her fists clenched, trying to still the frightening tumult within her. It always passed eventually, but she began to link the sensation with the friendly visits that were supposed to cheer her up.

When she couldn't stand it any longer, she said to David one evening, "I wish you'd call off your dogs, I've had enough company."

"A woman after my own heart," said he, for he didn't like droves of people marching in on him either.

She felt guilty because her desire to be by herself was prompted by a less worthy motive than the dignity of solitude. Yet she could not bring herself to tell him about these strange feelings that obsessed her. If I don't have to make the effort to talk to anyone, she thought, I'll be all right.

A whole day passed, and no one came to see her. She felt restless and unnerved. She tried to read, but the words on the printed page carried no meaning to her brain. She tossed the book aside, and rang for the floor nurse. Polly, who was on day duty, answered the call. Claudia asked her to lower the shade so that she could sleep.

"That's fine," said Polly, grateful, probably, to have one patient less to bother with. "I hope you have a nice long nap."

Claudia closed her eyes. A drum beat against her pillow. It was her heart beating. It beat so fast she couldn't breathe. Her skin felt too tight for her. If only she could walk around the room. She wondered what would happen if she did. The window was open. If she could stand by the window, perhaps she could breathe more easily. There was a weight on her chest, and it clamped her lungs so that she couldn't reach to the top of them. What a hideous feeling—this being hungry for air. She found herself looking at the window. A breeze was stirring the shade; it knocked gently against the sill. Nine stories down, automobiles were passing, and people were going about their business. Out in the corridor a baby cried. The morning paper lay beside her, with screaming headlines of the war. Suddenly it was as if space assumed dimension, and within the vastness, she was alone and lost. Fear strangled her. Her feet touched the floor. A thousand pins and needles ran up her legs, and drove her back to sanity. She cowered under the covers and groped for the bell.

Polly stuck her head in at the door. "Did you ring again, Mrs. Naughton?"

"Yes—I'm sorry—" she faltered. "Will you close the window and raise the shade?"

Polly laughed. "Am I crazy or did I just pull it down?"

Claudia bit her lips. Crazy. The word hit her with a new impact. She had never before realized that one's brain could be a greater source of agony than one's body. Asylums were full of crazy people, and sanitariums were full of people who had sick minds. Edith Dexter had been in a sanitarium after her son died. No one had ever said she was crazy, it was simply that she hadn't been herself for a time. I'm not myself either, thought Claudia. She had never thought about it before. Perhaps Polly would go out to the pantry, and whisper to the other nurses, "Mrs. Naughton in room 906 is a little queer, if you ask me."

"Is there anything else, Mrs. Naughton?"

"No, thanks." Claudia picked up the newspaper and held it in front of her, like a shield.

She put on another of the new nightgowns for David that evening, but he looked only at her face. "What's wrong, darling?"

She thought, He loves me too much. His love made her secretive and canny. "Don't you like this gown?"

"It's not the gown, it's you. Your voice is too cheerful for your eyes."

"You'd better get a new wife," she advised him flippantly.

"I don't want a new wife, I want this one." He

took her hands. "Listen, darling, this war won't last forever. We'll have another baby. We'll have lots of other babies."

She was silent, struck by the shocking realization that she had been absorbed neither in the horrors of the war nor the loss of her baby. For the moment nothing was important, except the aching awareness of her own being. Even David didn't seem real. She was glad when he went away, so that she could be alone with her misery and her shame.

He telephoned from Bridgeport in the morning, a quickly stolen moment to find out how she'd slept.

"Beautifully," she lied. "I feel fit as a fiddle."

"What kind of a fiddle?"

"A fiddle without a middle, but otherwise fine."

He must have felt her effort to be gay, for his quiet voice was like a gentle hand upon her. "Would you like to have the children come into town to see you this afternoon?" he asked her.

"Oh, David!" It was all she could say. Seeing the children would lend a meaning to the heavy hours that lay before her. They were symbols of a tangible achievement in a nightmare of frustration. She wondered how David had divined her need.

Exhilaration buoyed her up until she felt like a balloon floating at the top of the room, bumping the ceiling. "My but you're in a good humor," Polly remarked as she came in to give Claudia a sponge bath.

"My two boys are coming," said Claudia.

Polly was amazed. "I thought this was your first baby?"

"No," said Claudia tonelessly, "it would have been my third." Suddenly she was no longer dancing in the air. There was no buoyancy in her, only heaviness and despair.

"You certainly must have gotten married young," Polly continued. "And started right in, too."

"You make it sound very businesslike," Claudia murmured.

"Well, I mean, you know what I mean," said Polly. She flung the cloth that had bound Claudia's breasts with the pile of used sheets from the bed. "The doctor says we don't need this any longer. It's a relief, isn't it? I never can bear anything tight around me, myself. Say listen," she noticed abruptly, "I didn't mean to make you cry."

"You didn't. I'm just silly."

"You need diversion or something," Polly sagely advised. "How about a game of solitaire? I could borrow a deck of cards for you."

"I wouldn't know a spade from a club," said Claudia.

"For heaven's sake," said Polly. "I thought everyone played cards. Doesn't your husband either?"

Claudia shook her head. "He doesn't play golf, too."

"For heaven's sake," said Polly again. "No wonder you're moody."

Moody. Claudia thought about it after Polly had gone on to her next patient. She had never been moody in her life, she had never had any patience with moody people. But there was no denying now that she was up in the air one minute and down the next. She'd better get over these fits of temperament if she expected David to go on living with her. She must keep remembering that she had everything in the world to be grateful for. In two or three days she'd be getting up, and in another two or three days she'd be going home, where there'd be plenty to keep her busy. With the farm growing the way it was, Edward would be needing more help. She could learn to run the tractor now. There was no reason why she couldn't do a lot of things that would make her feel useful and important. I'll be perfectly all right, once I get home, she promised herself.

Having the children visit her was the next best thing to going home. She could scarcely wait for the knock on the door.

"Come in!" she called, and suddenly they were there, standing on the threshold with Jane. They all looked a little timid, as if they didn't know what to expect, as if they weren't quite prepared for what lay on the other side of the heavy hospital door. Claudia suddenly felt a little timid, too. Why did Matthew look so changed? Of course. She hadn't seen him since his haircut. Bobby looked different, too. Perhaps it was just because he was so clean, and buttoned up.

For a long moment nobody said anything. There was always a rift that lay between the sick and the well, it was like having to make friends all over again. Matthew was the first to break the silence. He said, with flat finality, "I want to go in the train again."

"That's a fine way to talk," Jane chided him. She drew him toward the bed. "Say a nice hello to your mother."

"Hello," said Matthew obediently.

"Hello," said Bobby, looking very self-conscious. "Aunt Julia sent me a game of croquet."

"That's wonderful," said Claudia. "I love croquet, I used to be an awfully good player."

"I can beat Jane already," he announced. He edged away from her, as if afraid that she was going to kiss him. She knew how he felt. Children hated to kiss people in bed. She wanted to help everybody, herself included, through these first awkward moments. "There's a nice spongecake on the bureau," she said. "And guess who made it?"

"Santa Claus," said Matthew, bored.

Jane laughed, as if he'd said something unusually clever. But Bobby said flatly, "You're a dope, Matthew."

"Bertha sent it," Claudia injected, feeling that it was all very anticlimactic and she should never have begun it. "Break off a piece each, for them, Jane, and some for yourself."

Jane removed her spotless chamois gloves, and according to the best tradition of spongecakes, broke the fluffy mixture without destroying its lightness. "It looks very nice," she conceded grudgingly. "Will you have some, Mrs. Naughton?"

Claudia winced at the mere thought of food. "No, thanks."

"You're peaked," said Jane critically. "You should be eating more. Here's your piece, Bobby. And don't spill the crumbs around."

"It has no icing," said Bobby, affronted.

"Spongecakes never do," Claudia told him. Personally there was no love lost between herself and a spongecake. She had always considered it one of those healthy confections, conceived in the era of elderberry wine and dyspepsia. She was willing to admit that a superior touch of craftsmanship was required in the perfect mixing and baking thereof, but as cakes went it was utterly sexless despite its dozen eggs. Being fully in accord with Bobby's indifference, she sought to re-engage his interest. "There are some lovely chocolate caramels on the desk," she tempted him. "Pass them around."

Matthew cleared his decks by gobbling his spongecake very quickly. He choked a little. Claudia was always a coward when it came to the children choking. Now the very tips of her fingers went numb with fright.

"He's all right," said Jane, lifting his arms above his head.

"He's a dope," said Bobby.

Jane compressed her lips. "That's a new word he's picked up in school," she explained in an aside to Claudia. "But he looks good anyway, don't you think so, Mrs. Naughton?"

"Yes, he does. . . . Matthew looks thinner, though, now that he's got ears."

"You have to get used to his not having curls," said Jane. "But it's plain to be seen he's got the makings of a handsome man," she added loyally.

"That dope?" Bobby queried in disdain.

The worm in Matthew turned. "I'm not a dope!" he hotly denied.

"Hush!" cried Jane. "I'm sorry I brought you, if you're going to act so naughty."

"Let's go home," Matthew suggested with alacrity. "I want to go in the train again."

Bobby nudged him. "You have to wait to see the baby," he said in a loud undertone.

Jane got very red. "Bobby! You mustn't say things like that!"

Bobby smiled in a superior sort of way, as if to say that he knew perfectly well that what had been going on for the last few months didn't add up to a spongecake and a box of caramels. Indeed, he remembered plainly that a visit to the hospital and some superior refreshments had also proceeded his initial introduction to Matthew.

"Didn't his father tell him?" Claudia asked faintly.

"Captain Naughton hasn't been able to get home but once, and the children were asleep. I'd have explained to Bobby myself, but I didn't think he noticed anything," said Jane, overcome with embarrassment.

Claudia knew that Jane's approach to all subjects pertaining to the birth of animal or human predated even the legend of the stork. Confronted with Bobby's clear-eyed stare, she would doubtlessly find herself involved in a fantastic tale concerning a small black bag that had inadvertently been mislaid by an absent-minded doctor. I'd better tell him now, thought Claudia. But it was hard to talk suddenly. A peculiar sensation assailed her. She felt as if her head were drifting off her shoulders. She heard herself say, from the other end of the room, "The baby died, Bobby."

Bobby looked at her mutely. For a long moment there was silence, except for Matthew making hay with the box of caramels. "Did you feel bad?" Bobby asked at last in a small voice.

Claudia's heart began to thump. It thumped all over her body. She tried to reassure him, to reconstruct the safety of his world, but her tongue lay thick and paralyzed against her lips.

"Of course Mother felt badly," Jane capably took over. "Now come along, it's time to go home."

All at once Bobby lost his air of superiority. His voice quivered, and he pulled at Jane's strong hand. "She's not going to die, too, is she?" he asked in a voice strangled with terror.

"Such nonsense!" Jane scolded him robustly.

"Such nonsense!" Claudia heard herself echo. "I'll be playing you a game of croquet before you know it, so you'd better practice up."

A load dropped visibly from Bobby's shoulders. He let go Jane's hand, and swung an imaginary mallet, keeping the pose as he followed the course of the ball across the room. "Whoopee!" he shouted.

"That looks to me more like golf," Claudia remarked with a remaining shred of coherence.

Jane laughed. "Come along," she said gayly, "or we'll miss our train." She, like Bobby, appeared to be tremendously relieved that the tenor of their lives had returned to normal; the loss of the baby had become an unhappy memory that belonged to the past. "Don't worry about anything at all, Mrs. Naughton. . . . Say a nice good-bye to your mother, Matthew."

"Hello," said Matthew perversely.

Claudia beat Bobby to it. "Dope," she whispered, with a little wink at him.

Bobby smiled, and then suddenly he leaned over the bed and kissed her.

Looking back upon it, from the dim jungle of the

days that followed, she felt that this moment was the trigger to her complete undoing. Bobby's kiss imposed upon her an obligation which she could not face, invested her with a strength she did not possess. She wanted to be the comforted, not the comforter; the child, and not the mother. All this came to her in a blinding flash of clarity which lasted but an instant and left confusion in its wake. She was two people, with two directions of thought which ran parallel without converging. She tried to bring herself together into one being, one thought, one feeling, but the effort was beyond her. Her body became an unruly dynamo of discord, and her separate minds grew disobedient to her will. She cried out in a frenzy against this cruel disruption of the smooth, whole person who had so short a time ago been Claudia Naughton. This, that she was going through, was a kind of death. It was worse than death, for there was no light to lead her out of the darkness, no hope of peace in her tortured brain. She understood why people jumped from windows.

Her shaking hand found the bell beneath her pillow. It seemed an eternity before Polly came trotting in. She gave a small gasp, and ran right out again. After a moment the superintendent of nurses appeared, full of starch and efficiency. Her fingers encircled Claudia's wrist, trying to catch her leaping heart. "Don't be alarmed," she said soothingly. "It's just a chill. We'll have you warm in no time." She gave a low order to Polly, who hovered in the background. "Send for Dr. Rowland, he's somewhere in the building."

A chill. Claudia had never had a chill before. The word was an injection of relief. A chill was something tangible to hold on to.

"It's pneumonia, isn't it?" she asked through chattering teeth, as Dr. Rowland stood looking down at her.

"Nonsense," he said. "We often run into a reaction of this sort. We'll get Miss Carey back for a few days, and keep you quiet. No visitors," he added firmly. "Not even your husband."

"Not even your husband." Strange. She loved David more than life itself, but she did not protest.

At the end of two weeks, Miss Carey announced cheerfully, "Surprise! We're going home this afternoon."

Claudia stared at her in dismay. "So soon?"

"So soon?" Miss Carey echoed in outrage. "Why you lazy good-for-nothing."

"Does my husband know?"

"No, it's a military secret."

"But he didn't mention it when he was here last night. Why didn't he?"

"Because we thought we'd wait and see how the weather was, and how you felt."

"I feel rotten," said Claudia glumly.

"Nonsense. You feel fine."

"I hate you."

"That's nice," said Miss Carey. "Give me those skinny legs of yours, I'll put your stockings on."

"There's no hurry. What time will the car be here?"

"What car?"

"Our car. Who's car do you think?"

"Humph," said Miss Carey. "You'll go in a train and like it. This is wartime."

"That's an excuse. You're taking me on the train because you think it's good for me. I'm on to your tricks."

"Smart, aren't you?" Miss Carey replied, which wasn't saying yes, and wasn't saying no.

"I suppose you think you're a wonderful nurse," Claudia taunted. "So tactful."

"I'm too good to waste on the likes of you," Miss Carey agreed. "Now get up, and no more back talk."

It was silly, but she went into a cold sweat before she was half dressed. Miss Carey, unperturbed, stuck some smelling salts under her nose. "Nothing to get scared about," said she. "You're just weak from lack of exercise."

"Then how am I going to get through a two-hour trip in a train?" Claudia demanded.

"You'll get through it. If you don't, I'm right there to sweep up the pieces and put them in the ash can."

A patient down the hall was going home at the

same time. Claudia, leaning on Miss Carey's arm, passed the open door. The girl was sitting in a wheel chair, in her hat and coat, and an older woman—her mother probably—was holding the baby with great pride. The baby wore a cap with a lace frill, which was not becoming to it's small red face. But the girl and the woman thought that the baby was beautiful —Claudia could tell that in one quick envious glance.

"Come along," said Miss Carey brusquely. "No post-mortems. The elevator's waiting. Keep stepping."

"Oh, shut up," said Claudia.

She knew that she could have never gotten through the trip if it weren't for the periodic hypodermics of Miss Carey's caustic banter. "I suppose," she remarked, shoving Claudia through a seething crowd of soldiers in Grand Central Station, "that you'd like me to sit down on the floor with you and take your pulse."

"It's the least you can do," Claudia retorted unsteadily, "it's hammering so I can hardly walk."

"You're managing a good imitation," said Miss Carey. "There's not one of these soldiers as handsome as your husband. I hope you realize that."

"I do," said Claudia, who wasn't thinking of David at that moment, but of how she was going to reach the train without collapsing.

"I'm seriously thinking," Miss Carey continued, "of having an affair with him."

"Go ahead," said Claudia. "See how far you get."

"I've got plenty of charm," said Miss Carey, "only I keep it hidden under my spectacles."

"I know you have," said Claudia. "You remind me of my mother."

Miss Carey thought about it. "Is there a dig in that?"

Claudia shook her head. "Not if you had known my mother," she said softly. It was strange how often she thought of her mother since she'd lost the baby. Sometimes she wondered if her mother and the baby were together. Sometimes she thought how nice it would be to look in on them some time. Crazy thoughts. She mustn't . . .

"This is rank extravagance," Miss Carey grumbled, as she presented her tickets to the gate conductor. "We don't need a drawing room."

"Eight cars down," said the conductor.

"Eight cars. I can't—" Claudia gasped.

"All right," said Miss Carey, shrugging. "It's nothing to me. Spend the night here for all I care." She dove into her purse, and withdrew the bottle of smelling salts. "Here," she said, "have a sniff of this—" She held the bottle under Claudia's nose. "Go on. Don't be so stingy. Take a big sniff."

"If anybody told me I'd be smelling smelling salts—"

Miss Carey pressed Claudia's clammy hand in her

warm, live grasp. "Never mind, you're doing an elegant job."

"Don't," said Claudia harshly. "If you pity me, I'll open my mouth and bawl. . . . What do you mean a drawing room is rank extravagance?"

"Your husband's doings. Not mine."

"I suppose you'd like me to stand all the way home?"

"It wouldn't hurt you. All you've done is loaf in bed. Let's see, this is the third car—only five more."

She never knew how she reached the drawing room. Miss Carey got her on to the sofa, and covered her with the blankets that an ebony-faced porter handed in at the door. "Lil lady don' feel good?" he queried solicitously.

"Lil lady don' feel good," Miss Carey granted. "Lil lady jackass, lil lady no-good white trash," she enlarged upon it, under her breath.

The porter shook his head, and his dark brooding eyes seemed to melt and roll down his creased cheeks. "She shuah do look powerful sick," he mumbled, as he shuffled out. "She sure do."

Claudia lay with closed eyes, trying to keep her body from dissolving into a craven, beaten pulp, trying to fight off the hideous evaporation of a concrete universe. Miss Carey sat beside her. "If you don't feel better in a little while, I'll give you some of that nice smelly medicine. But try to do without it, there's a good girl."

"I'll try." She opened her eyes. "Am I really powerful sick?" she whispered.

"No," said Miss Carey.

"Then what's wrong with me?" she cried in anguish.

"Nothing's wrong with you," said Miss Carey. "You've just lost step with the world for a little while. You'll catch up again."

Lost step with the world. She hadn't thought of it that way, but it was true. The world had rushed ahead while she tarried in some vast and lonely hinterland to meet for the first time the strangeness of her own soul. Now she wanted to find her way again, but she had lost the rhythm of life, she was no longer adjusted to the swift unconsciousness of being. The world was out of focus, it was as if she were seeing everything through a pair of glasses that were not fitted to her vision.

She had even lost step with the children, with Jane, with the farm itself. They were strangers meeting her at the door. The house looked unreal as if she had never been part of it; the cacophony of the barnyard assaulted her ears.

"Come and see my croquet set," Bobby demanded at once.

"Not now," Jane interpolated hastily. "Your mother's tired. She should rest before supper."

"I'll see it tomorrow," Claudia promised. She couldn't wait until she got upstairs to her own room.

She gave her weight to Miss Carey's strong, compelling arm.

Bobby followed them. "Why have you got a nurse?" he asked resentfully.

"I'm no nurse," said Miss Carey. "I've come to help with the farm.—Listen," she broke off, "I'd like to have a penny for every potato I've hoed, and every load of silage I've helped with." She stopped on the landing and filled her lungs with a big breath. "I smell manure," she announced ecstatically.

"Don't let Jane hear you say that; you're not supposed to smell it in the house," said Claudia.

"It's all over the place," Miss Carey insisted. "It's marvelous! I didn't know you had a real farm. I thought it was just a gentleman's hobby."

"It's a real farm," said Claudia wearily. "We even have our own bull now."

David telephoned a few minutes later. She talked to him, leaning white and spent against the pillows.

"Hello, darling—how does it feel to be home?"

"Lovely!"

"You don't sound it."

"I certainly do."

"I wish I could have called for you at the hospital. I couldn't get away."

"I know you couldn't."

"Did you stand the trip well?"

"Oh, fine. And thank you for the pretty drawing room."

"I picked out the nicest one I could find. With green cushions."

"Fine," she repeated inanely. She wished she could think of something else to say, but her brain was empty. Where was the spark that had always fired their conversations into a vaulting give-and-take, intelligible only to themselves? He, too, must have felt the lameness of her effort. "I'll see you at supper, darling. I'll try to be home by seven."

"I wonder," she said, as she put the instrument back on the table, "if he'd be very disappointed if I had a tray in my room."

"Over my dead body you're going to have a tray in your room," said Miss Carey decisively. She glanced at her watch. "I'll let you rest for exactly three-quarters of an hour."

"Thanks," said Claudia bitterly. "It'll serve you right if I have a heart attack."

"Go ahead and have it," said Miss Carey. "I'm going out and make friends with the bull."

"Keep it platonic!" Claudia yelled after her. It was odd and a little disturbing that she had come to be more at ease with Miss Carey, than with David. Miss Carey in some subtle way had seemed to supplant her need of him.

She felt even more keenly that this was true, during the endless ordeal of sitting up at the table for dinner. "This," said David, carving the thick steak, "is like old times." She supposed that it was, except for David's uniform, and Miss Carey's presence, and the festive luxury of caviar which Nancy Riddle had sent in lieu of a baby present.

Bobby sampled it distrustfully. "It's nasty, it's horrible!" he exclaimed with an elaborate shudder.

"Keep on thinking so," said David.

"I want some too!" Matthew demanded, spilling his glass of water.

Claudia wondered if their meals had always been so noisy, so nerve-wracking. And how could David carve with a hundred pounds of Great Dane pressing up on him at either side?

"Here," he said, presenting them each with a sliver of beef.

It was down before they tasted it. They looked all over for it in bewilderment, sniffling the rug and prowling under the table.

"They're imbeciles," David elucidated to Miss Carey. "Always have been. Always will be." He cut the tenderloin and put it on Claudia's plate.

"She'll eat about one tenth of that," Miss Carey said.

David laughed. "You don't know my wife's appetite."

Claudia let it pass. David didn't realize what food did to her now. "I'm too excited at getting home to eat much tonight," she excused herself. She couldn't even sample a piece of the lofty spongecake that Jane served, a little self-consciously, with the homemade ice cream. The cake spoke for itself. It was bigger and higher than Bertha's cake, by an inch around.

"Is that the kind you break?" Bobby demanded with disfavor.

"No remarks about food, young man," said David.

"Bobby's a dope," Matthew pleasantly injected.

It happened, then, in the fraction of an instant. Claudia felt herself splitting into two again. The scene was familiar, she had lived through it before, but she couldn't quite remember when, or where, or how. Confusion eddied around her, and swept her off from the safe, familiar shores of reason and serenity. Her heart leapt into her throat and pounded so hard that she could only reach in panic for breath. She pushed her chair back and stumbled blindly, dizzily from the room. Miss Carey rose to follow, but David said quickly, "No. I'll go—"

He lifted her and carried her up to her bed. Her hands were ice. There was no sensation in her limbs. He laid her against the pillows, and held her in his arms to warm her.

"I'm frightened," she sobbed wildly. "I'm frightened!"

"Darling," he whispered. "There's nothing to be frightened of."

He didn't understand. He didn't know what fear was. "Send Miss Carey," she implored him, "I've had these attacks before—she knows what to do for me. . . ."

David stood on the other side of the room, baffled and helpless, while Miss Carey took his place.

Eight

THAT NIGHT DAVID SLEPT IN THE ROOM THAT WAS TO have been the new nursery. Claudia was restless and wakeful, and twice she was aware of him listening anxiously at her door. Early in the morning, while the sun was still a faint gleam in the sky, he was there again. This time he was in uniform, grim reminder of a world at war. Yet by some beneficent whim of fate, her immediate universe was safe.

She often wondered, afterwards, how she could have been so ready to believe what she wanted to believe. It did not enter her head that David would not remain at Bridgeport indefinitely, and when on occasion he tried to prepare her for what was to come, she was too deeply entrenched in the battle of herself to realize what lay behind his words. Even on this first morning of her return from the hospital, it was an effort to focus him into reality. He was an intruder upon this intensely personal struggle for her own survival.

She had to force herself to let him know she was awake. He was at her side in an instant, a mutinous eye on the considerable hump of Miss Carey's solidly sleeping form in the adjoining bed. It was clear that he resented her being there, and he enacted with much gusto the gratifying procedure of ejecting her from the premises.

He was being funny about it, but Claudia recognized that he was more than half in earnest. He probably expected Miss Carey to be gone by suppertime. And why not? She'd never brought a nurse home from the hospital before. It hadn't been necessary. When Matthew was born, she'd started in the first morning to bathe and dress him, and within a week she was as good as new. Now there wasn't any baby to bathe and dress, and the business of putting her body together again was a slow and discouraging procedure. It was an exertion to so much as raise her head from the pillow.

"David," she whispered, "would you mind awfully if I kept Miss Carey a little longer?"

He was silent for a moment. Then he said gently, "Why of course not, darling. I was only joking. You keep her as long as you need her."

Her heart became still, and the knots at the back of her neck slowly untied. She slept.

When she opened her eyes, the room was bright with sunlight, and Miss Carey was standing by the bed with a tray. "Don't look so full of energy," Claudia said. "It exhausts me just to see you."

"Stop gabbling. Hurry up."

"Hurry up where? Why? For what?"

"Hurry up for to eat. Or are you one of those refined little slobs who don't wash their teeth before breakfast?"

"I always wash my teeth before breakfast. And what's more," Claudia continued stiffly, "I never have a tray in bed. I'd have to be half dead to eat in bed."

"Well, well, well," Miss Carey approved. "Maybe you're not such a bad sort after all. How'd you like to eat on the terrace wrapped up in a blanket?"

"I wouldn't like it at all," said Claudia. "I detest eating outdoors."

Miss Carey was mildly astonished. "I thought everybody loved to eat outdoors."

"Well, I don't," said Claudia. "And neither does David. We prefer the dining room without bugs and and caterpillars."

"That's a coincidence, so do I," said Miss Carey. "But I've always been ashamed to admit it." She started to go. "I'll keep everything hot in the oven until you're dressed."

"Come back here! Don't jump to conclusions!" Claudia shouted after her.

"Kindly make up your mind," said Miss Carey.

"I have. I'm not getting up."

"I thought you said you always did."

"I said I always did unless I'm half dead. Which I am."

"Sorry to disillusion you. You're the kind that lives forever."

"No, thanks."

"You won't get asked. Now hurry up and brush your teeth."

"I will not."

"So you are a slob," Miss Carey triumphed.

Claudia slipped down into the covers. "I'm not brushing, because I'm not eating. Now leave me alone."

"Listen," said Miss Carey, meaning business. "Would you care to have me hold your nose and pour this egg down your throat?"

"You sound like David," Claudia grumbled. "You'd have made a good husband for some woman."

"Failing that," Miss Carey ironically returned, "I'm a good aunt to half a dozen nephews. Would you believe this egg was still warm from the hen when I boiled it?"

"I think it's obscene. You could at least have let it cool off."

Nevertheless, she did away with half of it, and a swallow of orange juice. "When your stomach closes up against food, you just can't," she begged off. "Please take it away."

Miss Carey said, "I don't see how a man stands a wife who pecks at her meals, and vice versa. I'm glad I'm not married. Sour grapes." She carried the tray downstairs.

Claudia sank back against the pillows, and closed her eyes. She shouldn't have forced herself with the egg—it was doing horrid things to her. It was enough to make one afraid of eggs, afraid of orange juice, afraid of everything. That was the trouble—she was afraid, and the egg was merely something to hang her fear upon. She supposed everybody had to have things to hang their fears on. She remembered suddenly, how Roger lived in deathly fear of tomatoes, and Hartley was afraid of milk, in any form. I'm glad I have my egg, Claudia thought dryly. It was certainly better to be afraid of an egg, than to be afraid of fear. Last night she had been afraid of fear. She had been afraid because, while she was sitting at the table with her husband and her children, they had suddenly ceased to exist in relation to her. The universe had shredded into a vast unreality, and she had become a lost thing, groping in terror for an identity she did not possess. Now the same thing was happening. Fear was stealing in on her again, destroying her utterly, filling her limbs with ice and laying fire on her temples.

When Miss Carey returned from the kitchen a few minutes later, Claudia could scarcely speak. Miss Carey's voice reached her from a long way off. "This is a nice how-do-you-do," said she. "I turn my back for a minute and look at you."

"It's the egg," Claudia managed to explain with chattering teeth. "I was all right until I ate that egg."

Miss Carey made no reply. She found an extra blanket, and shook up the bottle of dark medicine that stood on the night table. "You must enjoy this smelly stuff," she remarked.

The dark smelly medicine was magic. It had a taste like old rags, but it sent the fear away. It helped her to go back into one piece, and brought the world into perspective again. "I loathe it," Claudia gulped. "But it makes me feel better. What's in it?"

"None of your business," said Miss Carey pleasantly. "But you're perfectly right," she added. "It is apt to lose its effect in time."

Claudia stared at her. "How did you know I was thinking that?"

"I know a lot of things."

"You know too much. What else, for instance?"

Miss Carey sat down on the edge of the bed. "Well, firstly," she began in a leisurely fashion, "you haven't got heart trouble. Or lung trouble. Nor yet stomach trouble. In short you're not going to die, as I believe I mentioned before."

"It's not death I'm afraid of."

Miss Carey nodded. "I know. It's just the dying. You want to be comfortable while you're about it."

"Yes, but even so, I don't mind a real good pain as long as it's real," Claudia tried to explain. "It's these hideous attacks that scare the wits out of me."

"Attacks!" Miss Carey jeered back at her. "You talk like an old lady with asthma."

"It's easy for you to laugh. You don't know what it's like."

"Oh. So you think you have a monopoly on funny feelings? You think you're the only person in the world who ever thought she was going crazy?"

Claudia could feel every muscle in her body tighten. Miss Carey was uncanny. She had penetrated Claudia's secret depths, there to uncover the agonizing fear that lay at the bottom of all her fears. It was something she was afraid to acknowledge even to herself. It was idiotic, of course, but she kept remembering that fall on her head last summer—the time she had saved the little colored girl. Perhaps it had left her with some injury to her brain that was accountable for these queer feelings. She wet her dry lips. "How can I be sure I'm not going crazy?" she stammered.

"Because people who think they are never do."

"You're just saying that to make me feel better. How can you possibly know?"

"First hand experience."

Claudia sat up in bed. "You mean you've been like this?"

"Much worse."

"I don't believe it."

"It's something people don't go around bragging

about. At the same time, it's really quite a unique privilege. . . . Only you won't be able to see that until you're all through with it. Graduated, and gotten your diploma."

"Be serious!"

"I am."

"But how did it start with you?"

Miss Carey shrugged. "One day I was God Almighty, and the next day I was a bundle of sniveling fears and aches and pains."

"Like me," Claudia breathed. "What did you do?"

"Gave up nursing for six months, put a sign out on my head, 'Closed for repair', and spent all my savings on doctors' bills—Oh, I got my money's worth, all right. I ended up by losing a perfectly good gall bladder and two molars, to say nothing of a pair of tonsils and what remained of my self-respect."

"You've a nerve to kick as long as you're cured," said Claudia enviously.

"I'd have been just as cured if I'd gone in for a love affair or Christian Science."

"I'm not the type for either. What lies in between?"

"Hell," said Miss Carey briefly. "Plain unadulterated hell. Only don't be afraid of it."

"How can I help being afraid of it?"

"You'll learn to handle it."

"How?"

"How, how, how. I don't know how. That's one

of the things you'll have to learn for yourself. Nobody can help you. Not even your husband."

"Least of all, my husband. He's never known fear in his life."

"Funny," said Miss Carey, reflectively, "I'd have said the opposite."

"Why?"

"Oh I don't know. Once you've been initiated to this particular brand of torture, it's a kind of secret society. You can spot a fellow-member a mile off."

Claudia fell silent. Her thoughts went back again to last summer. It was just about the time she'd almost been run over, that David had worried her so. She remembered how she had had to handle him with kid gloves. For weeks on end, he hadn't been himself—depressed and edgy and given to scratching his head before he went to sleep at night. But no. It couldn't be. He'd been worried about tangible things, such as money and business, and the war.

"How do trains run up here, by the way?" Miss Carey broke in upon her.

"They run all right," said Claudia absently.

"Good. I'd like to get one before supper."

"What for?"

"I like to ride in trains before supper."

"Don't be silly. Where to?"

"Back to town, where do you think?"

"But you're staying on—"

"To do what? Hold your hand and tell you what a fine girl you are?"

"You can help with the farm. You said you loved farming and you're strong as an ox."

"You do manage to make me feel graceful and feminine," said Miss Carey. "Be that as it may, however, I'm pretty expensive farm-labor."

Claudia was abashed to say "I need you," so she said instead, "David said you should stay."

"Your David," Miss Carey remarked without rancor, "will be very happy to see the last of me."

Claudia wondered whether Miss Carey had used mirrors earlier that morning to catch his uncomplimentary pantomime. "He likes you," she defended. "He thinks you're a very civilized person."

"And I think he's an extremely wise young man," Miss Carey returned. "I take my hat off to him."

"So do I," said Claudia slowly. She did not have to ask Miss Carey what she meant. It was something that could not be put into words. It was as if already some small measure of pure knowing had been crystallized out of the confusion of the past few weeks. She realized suddenly that all marriage held the seeds of tragedy, and love needed eternal vigilance. At this strange crossroads of her life, it would be easy, deadly easy, for Miss Carey to slip into David's place. Miss Carey knew it. David knew it. And now, finally, Claudia knew it.

"If you're going to leave," she said huskily, "it

would be easier if you didn't wait until suppertime."

Miss Carey, who was on her way out of the room with the bottle of smelly medicine, came back and stood by the bed. She took Claudia's hand in both of her own. "Do people by any chance think you're a fool?" she quietly asked.

"Only fools," said Claudia.

David couldn't get home for supper that night. It was ten o'clock before Claudia heard the car drive into the garage. A moment later, the heavy door closed down and his firm step hurried up the path toward the terrace. Her heart quickened and her hands were cold as ice. She was as nervous, she thought impatiently, as a schoolgirl meeting her lover. She felt gauche, too, and a little clumsy in her attempt to re-establish the reckless idiocy with which they were wont to meet after the briefest separation. . . . "Anyone can be passionate," she'd once remarked, "but it takes real lovers to be silly." Now, at this moment, she was neither. She could only pretend a joy in seeing him, and the little note that she had placed on his bed, "VACANCY—INQUIRE NEXT DOOR," was a heavy-handed imitation of her usual style.

For a long moment, David stood looking at the sign. Then he knelt beside her, and laid his cheek against her hair. "Be patient with yourself, darling."

"How long can you be patient with me?" she asked him in a low voice.

"Don't worry about that."

"I'm so shaky," she faltered.

"That's natural. You've had a shock to your psyche and a shock to your physical system. Besides, you've been through one thing and another ever since you lost your mother. You've got to expect to take a little time off to get yourself straightened out."

"Is that what Dr. Rowland told you?"

"I don't need anyone to tell me. Didn't you always say I should have been a doctor?"

She nodded. She wanted to blurt out, "David, did you ever feel like jumping out of a window because you couldn't face another day?" But her courage deserted her. She had everything in the world to be grateful for. How could she blast his illusion of her by confessing that life had become intolerable? How could she make him understand that it was her failure as a woman, and not his failure as a man? "I'll be human again one of these days," she promised unsteadily.

"Of course you will. Oh and by the way, I rated three hours' extra leave tomorrow. We can have breakfast together. I don't have to report until eleven."

"That's wonderful," said Claudia.

He kissed her. "It's late, darling. Turn around and go to sleep. I'll get undressed in the bathroom."

Gratitude filled her. She put her arms around him. "David, I love you so."

"I love you too," he answered.

It was odd that they should suddenly find it necessary to express their love in words. In all the years of their marriage, they had never needed speech. He must have felt strange about it too, for he stood looking down at her, a little alien, a little at a loss. Then he bent to kiss her again, and pulled the blanket up over her shoulder—a habit borrowed from herself. It was what she always did when she kissed the children good night. "Call me if you need anything," he said.

"I won't need anything. I feel fine," she assured him, with a sudden lift of mood. To her joy, she discovered that she actually did feel quite at ease. Ease was the opposite of disease, she suddenly realized. One felt at ease when one's mind and body and soul were in attunement. While she was thinking about it, she fell asleep.

The heavy beating of her heart wakened her sharply. Panic was upon her before she could ward it off. She sat up reaching for breath. When her heart beat like that, it pounded the breath out of her. That was what frightened her, she couldn't breathe. The walls of the room were closing in on her. Sometimes they shredded away, sometimes they closed in. Now, in the darkness, they were closing in. She wished she had not let Miss Carey go, for David wouldn't know what to do for her. She didn't want him to even know that she was awake, he needed his sleep. She crept stealthily from the bed and felt her way across the room against the looming obstacles of mantel and dresser, unfamiliar and threatening in the blackness. It seemed an eternity before she felt the knob of the bathroom door within her hand. She turned it slowly, pressing hard against it, to keep it from creaking. She switched on the bathroom light, first taking care to close the door again. Her face stared back at her from the medicine chest mirror, filled with the sickness of fear, and pale. She thought, I can't look this way in the morning, I have to have breakfast with David. Her hand shook as she reached for the bottle of dark medicine.

Either she was used to the blackness, or dawn was beginning to lighten the sky, for she made her way swiftly and noiselessly back to the bed. She must remember what Miss Carey had said: she didn't have heart trouble, and she wasn't going crazy. She must keep on remembering, until the medicine started to work. . . . Then the medicine would take over where Miss Carey had left off. She felt like a tightrope walker, trying to reach solid ground.

"Are you all right dear?"

It was David's quiet voice from the other bed. So he had been awake all the time. "I just wanted a drink of water," she lied. She was angry at him for forcing her to tell him an untruth. He had no right to be awake. He loved her too closely. It was better to be like most married couples. Julia had once said that she could cry her eyes out all night, and Hartley would sleep right through. It was a comfortable way to live. She began to see why married couples often had separate bedrooms if they could afford it. But David didn't even like separate beds. She thought in a kind of wonder, I didn't either, until I lost the baby. . . . She clenched her fists and waited for the medicine to bring her sleep.

It was a different kind of sleep, torpid and conscious, as if only a part of her lay sleeping. Her brain was awake long before her heavy lids could lift. Her brain said to her this morning, "The medicine worked, you feel all right." She heard the hum of the household going on, the dogs barking, Bobby getting ready for school. She opened her eyes and looked toward the other bed. David was asleep. She was glad.

Jane thought that he had left for Bridgeport as usual. She looked startled when she came to the door with Claudia's tray. "Is he sick?" she whispered.

He stirred and stretched. It wasn't a sick man's stretch. Before he was fully awake, Jane, who sometimes thought very fast, appeared with a second tray. His masculinity was outraged. "I'll get up and eat it on the desk," he compromised, but Claudia coaxed him to have it in bed. "I won't tell the Army on you," she said.

"I have to get up and wash my teeth first anyway," he argued.

"Nonsense. That's just a self-imposed tradition. I didn't yesterday, and I was surprised how it didn't matter."

"You're not me," he said, fishing for his slippers. "This is more than a tradition."

Bobby came in. He was ready for school, and in a hurry. "Good-bye!" he greeted his mother feverishly. "I have to go! I'm late! The bus is coming." He caught sight of the other tray on the rumpled bed. "Is the nurse back again?" he demanded, with a scowl like David's.

"Didn't you like Miss Carey?" Claudia asked him curiously.

"I like you to be up," he answered, with no regard for Miss Carey one way or the other. "I don't like it when you have to stay in bed."

"You certainly are a slave driver," said Claudia lightly.

"You promised to play me a game of croquet," he reminded her.

"I will. This afternoon. . . . Now run and knock on the bathroom door and tell Miss Carey breakfast is ready."

"I haven't got time," said Bobby. "The bus is coming, I have to be out in front. It's a rule."

"It's also a rule to obey your mother," said Claudia firmly. "I asked you to tell Miss Carey her breakfast is getting cold. Besides, there's no sign of the bus yet. It's too early."

"It's not," said Bobby, at whose stage of life nothing was too early. "I'll be late," he warned her ominously, as he banged on the bathroom door with an urgent fist. "Miss Carey!" he shouted hoarsely. "My mother says to tell you breakfast is ready!"

David's high falsetto sounded from within. "Yes, dearie, I'll be right out!"

Bobby was much too much in a hurry to notice the highly inaccurate imitation of Miss Carey's deep contralto. "She'll be right out," he relayed over his shoulder. "I have to go now. Good-bye!"

The bathroom door opened, and David's hairy arm blocked his precipitate exit. "Hey!" Bobby protested indignantly, and then made believe he'd known it was David all along.

"Oh ho! Yes you did!" David gloated. "Like fun you did!"

"Daddy's a sissy, Daddy's eating breakfast in bed!" Bobby retaliated in high glee. "Why are you home?" it occurred to him to question belatedly. Apprehension caught at him. "Aren't you in the Army any more?"

"They wouldn't have me," said David, looking very glum.

Bobby was gullible, for all he pretended not to be. His face fell. If his father were no longer a member of the armed forces, that was ignominy, indeed—second only to the inglorious convenience of his being stationed at Bridgeport. "Can't you even wear a uniform?" he asked in a stricken voice.

David took pity on him. "I was only joking, dummy. I've got a couple of hours off."

"I knew they didn't kick you out!"

"You know a lot," David retorted. "Put your belly button in. Don't you ever close your shirt?"

"I did," said Bobby, "it opens."

"Now you've buttoned it wrong," said Claudia. Bobby unbuttoned his shirt, only to rebutton it askew.

"Come over here," said David. "Now get conscious. Find your top button and your top button hole, and work down. Go on—let me see you do it."

Bobby grinned, debating the advisability of provoking parental authority. He decided against it.

"Now let's see your nails," David continued sternly.

Bobby docilely gave his hand and then, with David's own technique, adroitly clipped his father's nose.

"So." David's voice was full of ominous portent. He set his tray aside. A lamp fell over, but it didn't break. "Hoodlums!" cried Claudia, thinking how wonderful it must be to have so much energy so early in the morning. She thought, I'm glad they're so close.

It was good for a father to have a son, and for a son to have a father, and to be friends. They did not even hear the school bus come lumbering down the road. After a moment Jane came rushing into the room. "Bobby!" she cried in agitation, "The bus is waiting, hurry up." She carried his lunch box and a thin sweater. She pulled the sweater over his head. He thrashed the air. "It's too hot!" he protested violently. "Do you want me to suffocate?"

"It's not that hot," said Jane. "And mind you don't trade your good sandwiches for the Lord knows what."

"All the boys trade."

"Then I'll make you a trade-sandwich of jelly," said Jane. She put up her nose. "Bologny indeed. That's what he gives up good roast beef for, Mrs. Naughton, bologny, without butter or lettuce or anything!"

The bus blew its horn warningly before Bobby could argue the superiority of bologny over beef, with or without the concentrated nourishment that Jane managed to pile between two unsuspecting slices of bread. "I have to go," he averred, and this time there was no urgency in his voice, no pressure to be off. "I'll see you tonight," he said. He flung his arms around Claudia in a quick hug and butted his head into his father's chest. "See you tonight," he repeated, jauntily. He looked back at them from the door. His world had returned to normal. It was a pleasant world to leave, because he knew it would be there to come back to. "Good-bye!" he said again.

"Good-bye!" said Claudia and David in a single voice. They looked at each other and smiled, tasting vicariously this suspended moment of childhood with all its myriad implications. "But I wouldn't want it over again," said David elliptically. "I'm glad I am where I am."

"I'd want it," said Claudia. Her mind went back to her mother and herself. How secure, how safe those years had been. "How can you say it isn't wonderful to be a child?" she questioned David almost angrily. "No obligations, no responsibilities, no conflicts."

"Grow up," said David. "Besides, children are too dependent on adults. I lived through some rotten times on account of my parents."

"We're not that kind of parents."

"How do we know?"

"I never thought of that," said Claudia.

A disturbance in the lower hall drowned their discussion into silence. Bobby, on the way out, had discovered the inexplicable absence of his arithmetic book from his schoolbag. It was a major tragedy. More than that, it was a vicious plot. People stole his book. He wasn't accusing Jane directly, but she had doubtless had a hand in the conspiracy.

"No such thing!" they heard Jane indignantly deny. "You must have left it someplace as usual. I gave you a clean handkerchief. That's gone, too. What did you do with it?"

"Here they are!" David shouted, spying them on the foot of his bed. Jane flew upstairs like the White Queen, and flew down with Bobby in her wake. Claudia could hear the clatter of her heels on the stone path as she deposited him personally in the bus. It chugged heavily and moved on. The Danes ran after it, barking ferociously and biting at its rear wheels, knowing very well that they couldn't bite back. David took a deep breath. "Is it always like this?" he asked.

"Always," said Claudia limply. "You're never home at this hour. You've no idea."

"Something should be done."

"There's nothing. We've tried."

"It'll shorten Jane's life."

"It's already shortened mine." She meant it, although she tried to look as if she didn't. The smile on her face was wooden, and her gayety forced. The effect of the medicine she had taken before dawn was wearing off and unreality was stealing over her again. There was a kind of dishonesty in lying there, pretending to be her smiling self, when she was careening off into space, in search of a oneness that she could neither find nor hold. David must have sensed the panic that was stirring in her, for he leaned over, and caught her hand and lifted it to his lips. "Brace up," he said, "here comes the second contingent."

It was Matthew sidling through the door. Matthew was devious, alternately fiend or angel, according to his wants. This morning he was purely angel, as he drifted between their beds and embraced them in an impartial smile. He felt no responsibility in their personal problems, and although he had never known his father to have his breakfast in bed, he did not question the departure.

"Why does Jane dress him in pale blue?" demanded David, who had a horror of either of his sons being less than virile.

"Tweeds might be a little elderly," Claudia remarked, "considering he's only two."

"So he is," David allowed. He hadn't quite learned to be friends with Matthew. Matthew belonged to Jane, Matthew was happy in the kitchen, Matthew lived solely for his own ends.

Now David regarded him in slight embarrassment. But Matthew felt no reservations. He turned on all his lure, and slipped his hand into his father's with disarming sweetness. Claudia saw David's face contort. "I only hope," he said, "that this is honey."

"It must be," Claudia placated him. "He has it at breakfast sometimes."

"It's a menace," said David, "to the walls and furniture." He dipped his napkin into the glass of water on his tray, and removed the sticky aura that clung to Matthew's fingers. "He has my hands," he discovered blandly.

Claudia agreed. "I always said so. And he's going to have the back of your neck too."

"Let's see you make a fist," said David.

It was a foolish fist, no more than crumpled rose petals. David, however, was gratified. "See," he showed Claudia, "he's got his thumb out."

"Is that good?"

"Perfect. Only girls make fists with their thumbs in. Come on, you scalawag, I'll show you how to box."

They pranced around the room, boxing. It seemed that the room couldn't be noiser, and then suddenly it was. Bluff and Bluster, having returned from chasing the bus, decided that the center of activities on this particular morning was taking place on the upper floor. Clumsily, and with a great deal of commotion, they manipulated the stairs, and presented themselves with a triumphant wriggling of their gigantic bodies. Bluster's wagging tail caught Matthew in an unexpectedly vulnerable part of his anatomy, and caused him to double up in startled dismay. David winced in sympathy. "Ouch," he murmured. "That hurts." It was the final bond between them.

The house was very quiet after David left. "It's too nice to stay indoors," said Jane with Miss Carey's instructions sticking out from under her wheedling tone.

"All right," said Claudia listlessly.

Spring had come in the short space of time she had been in the hospital. The big maple beside the terrace was wearing its new leaves in a matter of fact fashion, and Claudia thought of how she and Jane had planned for the baby to lie beneath its shade. She walked toward the barn, away from the tree. The tree hurt.

Edward stopped what he was doing when he saw her. "It's nice you're around again, Mrs. Naughton," he said diffidently. He showed her Ruby's latest litter of pigs. There were twelve of them, complete and sufficient. Ruby puts me to shame, thought Claudia. She couldn't wait until she got out of the barn.

She stood in the sunshine, feeling anew the emptiness of her body and the dim aching of her useless breasts. It was as if losing the baby had cost her her place in the great scheme of things, and she felt more acutely than ever that queer sense of having lost step with the universe. She sought Jane out in the kitchen and asked her for something to do.

Jane said, "I was just wishing for someone to shell me some peas."

Claudia made a face. Shelling peas was a task that insulted even Matthew's limited capabilities. Yet after ten minutes of it, she felt drained of vitality and purpose. The heap of tiny green globules floated before her vision in mammoth distortion, and her hands grew fumbling. She pushed back her chair and said, "I'll be back in a minute." Jane could draw her own conclusions.

In a little while, Jane went in search of her. Claudia heard her step on the stairs. She rose swiftly from the bed, and pretended to be straightening her bureau drawers.

"Oh," said Jane, relieved. "I thought maybe you didn't feel well."

"I feel fine," said Claudia. She wondered how she could go on hiding her despair behind this monstrous lie.

For the second time in succession, David could not get home for supper that evening. The children went to bed, disappointed, their day uncrowned. Claudia realized that she had grown apart from them. Perhaps they sensed that she was not there to fill their need.

She knew that this must not happen between herself and David. David must come home and find her waiting for him. The sign that she had made the night before was still in the table drawer. She took it out, and stuck it back upon his pillow. Only now, she lifted the pillow onto her bed, beside her own.

He came at long last, and his arms were around her. She said, knowing it, but not feeling it, "You'd be surprised how handsome you are in uniform."

Later she said, with her heart pounding up into her throat, "You're handsome in pajamas, too."

He looked at her for a moment without answering. Then he unpinned the sign from his pillow, and put the pillow back on the other bed.

"Go to sleep," he said, gently. He kissed her, and switched the room into darkness.

She wept, because there was no feeling in her except relief.

The next night he suggested that it might be better if he slept in the other room so as not to disturb her when he got up in the morning. She wanted to say, "Don't be silly." But she could only look at him, mute with gratitude.

Dr. Rowland had told her that he wanted to see her in a few weeks for a final examination. She kept putting it off, and David kept reminding her. He arranged, one day, to drive her to town, and then at the last minute, he telephoned from Bridgeport that he couldn't get away. "Jane'll go in the train with you," he said.

"And leave who with the children? Don't you think I can be trusted to go by myself?" She spoke with more bravado than she actually felt. The prospect of the long train ride filled her with foreboding. It was utterly ridiculous, but there it was.

Jane hovered about her while she dressed. Her clothes hung on her. "I look like a scarecrow," she said.

"Many's the woman would be glad to have no shape like you," Jane declared. "We need some dish towels and some socks for the children in case you get around to shopping."

Claudia decided that it was a salute to the actress in her that Jane could possibly think that she would have either the energy or the courage to drag herself into a store. Already her heart was beginning to pound against her ribs, and little drops of chill moisture were trickling down the undersides of her arms. What a horrid feeling. And she used to be so proud of herself because she never perspired. David had always insisted that it was nothing to be proud of, but she couldn't help feeling that it was. I'm certainly making up for lost time now, she thought, as she changed to a fresh blouse.

The dogs bounded out to escort her to the car. She cowered against the gate. "Get away!" she cried. "You'll knock me over!"

Edward, who was driving her to the station, thought that she was joking. He laughed easily and said, "They're big fellers all right." Only the dogs seemed to know that her knees were shaking. They edged off from her, uncertain and a little puzzled by her rebuff. I'm getting to be afraid of everything, she realized miserably.

She met Elizabeth Van Doren at the station. Elizabeth said, "How nice. I'm going into town, too."

A suspicion entered Claudia's mind. Perhaps David had asked Elizabeth to go with her. She wanted to find out the truth of it, but Elizabeth's calm face told her nothing, and she was afraid to ask. She found herself talking gayly, brightly, above the grinding of the wheels. She was like another person, listening to herself. "I'm wound up. I can't stop." David couldn't stand talkative women. She dug her nails into the palms of her hands. She made herself keep quiet. There was a time when she had felt sorry for Elizabeth. Now Elizabeth was probably the one who was feeling pity.

"My dental appointment isn't for another hour. I could go with you to the doctor," Elizabeth offered casually as the train drew in at the terminal.

Claudia laughed. "How ridiculous," she said. She loved Elizabeth, but she wanted to get away from her. She couldn't wait until she got into a cab by herself. But when the cab drew up in front of Dr. Rowland's office, she was so dizzy that she asked the driver to help her up the stoop.

Miss Kennedy opened the door for her. It all seemed to have happened once before. The familiar cloud of unreality settled upon her—she fought against it, but she could neither isolate nor conquer the sensation. It might have been minutes or hours later that she found herself seated in the chair beside Dr. Rowland's desk.

He settled the eternal flower in his buttonhole. He said, referring to her history chart, "Let me see, this baby was expected toward the end of June?"

"The fourteenth," said Claudia.

He glanced at her. "Don't feel too badly. With this dreadful war, perhaps it's all for the best." He ad-

justed the blood pressure machine around her arm.
"Is your husband overseas yet?"

"No," said Claudia. "He won't be sent. He's stationed here."

"That's very nice," said Dr. Rowland. "A young
architect friend of mine just went over with some
troops. He sailed from San Francisco." He unwound
the tape, and put the machine aside. "How do you
feel in general, Mrs. Naughton?"

"Not too well," she admitted unsteadily.

"Dizzy? Tired?"

She nodded, appalled lest this terrifying insecurity
had grown conspicuous. Perhaps it was apparent in
her face. Perhaps her eyes looked wild and strange.
Perhaps everyone who saw her discerned at once that
she was on the verge of going to pieces. She had to
know the truth about it. Her lips moved woodenly.
"How do you know?"

"With a blood pressure of eighty-two it's not surprising," he said.

A weight lifted from her heart. There was a physical reason for her to feel as she did. Her symptoms
weren't in her head, she wasn't imagining them. They
were real and reliable, and therefore to be respected
and not ignored. "I can't eat," she unburdened in a
rush. "And I'm down to a hundred and four pounds."

"Humph," said Dr. Rowland, thinking about it.
"In that case, you'd better have a thorough going
over. A basal metabolism and a series of abdominal

X-rays." He wrote the names of several physicians on his prescription pad. "Also a complete checkup of your teeth."

Claudia stared at him. Surely he couldn't be in earnest. Surely this was some private joke between Miss Carey and himself. But no. He was deadly serious. He gave her the slip of paper and said, "I'd attend to this as soon as possible if I were you. As for my examination, I find everything perfectly normal, you can go on as usual."

"Thank you," said Claudia. At the door she turned. "Where can I reach Miss Carey? I'd like to see her."

"She's on a case in Greenwich."

"Oh," said Claudia, disappointed.

Out in the street she made her own decision. She tore the slip of paper into tiny pieces. Then she called a cab and bought some dish towels and the children's socks.

She merely told David that evening that Dr. Rowland's examination had found her perfectly recovered. "He said I could go on as usual."

"Good," said David. "I called him, but he'd left his office." He looked at her closely. "Is everything else all right?"

"My blood pressure's down, that's all." It had already become a prop to lean upon. She thought, I wouldn't give up my low blood pressure for a million dollars. She was grateful to the point of exhilaration.

She found it quite easy to say, when David bent to kiss her good night, "Don't you think it's time we weren't so stylish any longer? I think we've had separate rooms long enough."

"High time," he agreed. "Also very opportune."

"Why opportune, of all words?"

"I was keeping it as a surprise."

"Tell me now," she broke in.

"I'm going to get a ten day furlough."

She was amazed. "Already?"

"That's not very complimentary."

"But I thought it would be ages before you'd get a decent leave."

"So did I," he said shortly.

"When does it start?"

"The beginning of June."

"That's only a few days off!—I think it's simply darling of the Army," she hastened to add.

"Very darling."

"You don't seem happy about it, though."

"I am."

"The weather will be lovely, we'll have lovely times." She was aware as she spoke, that it was with the perfunctory enthusiasm of a hostess planning a pleasant weekend for a guest. He caught her by the shoulders. "What's in your thoughts?" he asked her gruffly.

"Nothing," she stammered. Did he divine the prayer within her heart? "Dear God, let me feel all right for David's vacation, let me be to him what a wife ought to be. . . ."

"Nothing," she repeated. "What's in your own thoughts?"

"Nothing," he said.

They both knew that they were lying to each other.

On the day before his furlough started, she drove down to the village for a manicure and a shampoo. She drove slowly, like a novice, with her eyes peering anxiously ahead, and both hands stiff upon the wheel. She tried to relax, to recapture the old happy-go-lucky method of driving that had never failed to arouse David's ire. But by the time she pulled up in front of Glorianna's BEAUTY SHOPPE, her face was pallid and drawn with strain.

She hadn't been inside of the shop since last summer. Glorianna was waiting for her. She gave a start when she saw her walk in. "Goodness," she said, "I hardly recognized you, Mrs. Naughton. You look simply fine," she hastened to add.

"You'll never go to heaven," said Claudia, sinking into a chair. "Do something to me, Glorianna. I want to look nice for tonight."

"Are you going to the dance at the Club?" Glorianna asked with lively interest.

"No, I'm having company," Claudia answered.

Glorianna examined one of Claudia's hands. "Oh, your nails are much better!" she effused.

"I'm not doing much outside work this year," Claudia explained. She picked up a tattered magazine. It was all so much like last year. Except that last year she had been a different person. It was impossible to believe that she, who had been friends with herself from the day she was born, should now be experiencing this terrifying split in the harmony of her body and her mind. There was no peace in the world, and there was no peace in her own soul. Perhaps one had to do with the other. The thought was too big for her. That was part of the trouble, big thoughts kept coming to her, thoughts that were too strong for her to handle. They threw her overboard to flounder beyond her depth. Now, at this very moment, she was floundering. Her heart beat so heavily that she was sure that Glorianna must hear it pounding in her breast. She tried to cover her discomfort with nonchalance. "Do you still go in for astrology?" she asked.

Glorianna shook her head. "No, I gave it up," she said. "I'm in Unity now. Do you know anything about Unity?"

"No," said Claudia.

Glorianna withdrew a very small paper volume from her apron pocket. Claudia glanced at the opening page. It was largely about God. Everybody has to have something, she thought. She envied Glorianna with her small business, and her ability to shift from one prop to another.

"I had a nervous stomach all year," Glorianna volunteered. "Unity helped me a lot."

"You're fortunate," said Claudia.

"Do you ever see Mrs. Riddle?" Glorianna continued conversationally. "She was in yesterday. She's got four English sailors for a week."

"That's nice," said Claudia.

"Mrs. Van Doren comes in once in a while, too. She's awfully sweet, isn't she?"

"Very."

"It's a shame she's a widow. Honestly. The trouble there is in this world. Now if you'll sit over here, I'll give you a nice facial before I wash your hair."

"I never had a facial."

"You'll love it. It makes such a difference in your skin. And when I shampoo you, I'm going to give you a light rinse."

"Oh, no," said Claudia, "Please."

Glorianna laughed. "It's not a bleach, or anything! It just brings out all the high lights. Now just relax."

Claudia put her head back and closed her eyes. "Go ahead. Anything to make me look better," she wearily agreed.

Two hours later, Glorianna, who was painstaking, if not inspired, stood off and viewed her handiwork. "Now you can see yourself," she said with pride.

Claudia saw herself. "Oh dear," she said.

"You'll like it a lot better tomorrow," Glorianna told her optimistically. "Your wave'll loosen up, and a facial always looks better the second day, too."

"But I wanted to use my hair and my face tonight," Claudia reminded her unhappily.

"You only imagine it's not nice," said Glorianna. "You just wait until your husband sees you. He'll think you're the prettiest woman at your party."

"I don't doubt it," said Claudia.

Bobby was playing croquet with himself when she rolled into the driveway. He dropped his mallet and ran over to her. "I beat two games," he announced. "Do you want to play me?"

"Some other time. I'm tired, dear."

"That's what you always say," he told her resentfully. "You never play with me. . . . Daddy'll be home for his vacation tonight, won't he?" he went on, following a train of thought.

"Yes," said Claudia.

"Boy," said Bobby in simple ovation.

"Boy, what?"

"We'll go swimming and fishing and boxing and everything. You look funny," he noticed abruptly. "Your hair is funny."

She bit her lips. "Please don't be fresh."

"I'm not fresh. You don't look nice," he insisted.

Rage filled her. She slapped him. He was stunned and affronted. "I don't like you," he shrieked.

She slapped him again, and he kicked her. They stared at each other in a kind of horror. Claudia felt helpless and frustrated. She began to cry. Bobby was frightened. He began to cry, too. Claudia ran blindly into the house, and Bobby went back to his croquet game. Claudia saw him from her bedroom window. He wasn't playing any longer. He was pounding the ground with his mallet. She turned quickly and locked herself in the bathroom. For the first time in weeks, she took a teaspoonful of the dark medicine. Then she stuck her head in a basin of water and washed out the punctilious wave and the reddish rinse. After that she went downstairs, to make her peace with Bobby. "I'm sorry I slapped you," she said.

He looked up from his lessons. Her apology flustered him. He kicked at the table with the toe of his boot. "That's lovely for the table," said Claudia. He smiled sheepishly. By the time David came home, everything seemed as usual.

He moved back into their bedroom that night. He held her closely, and she said she was happy. But when his lips touched her cheek, he must have known that she was crying. She wanted to apologize to him, as she had apologized to Bobby. She wanted to be there for him, but she knew that she had failed him. He could not find her, because she could not find herself. Her soul was shipwrecked on the remote island of her fears.

That night, just as dawn was beginning to trail pale fingers across the inky sky, pain came to her. It was a full and engrossing pain that made her forget everything else but pain. She sat up in bed, doubled over with it. It began somewhere in the deep center of her, and bore through her in all directions, laying the great sickness of it in the small of her back.

"What is it, dear?" David asked from his bed.

She did not answer. She wanted him to think she was asleep. Tomorrow—this morning—was the beginning of his vacation. She mustn't spoil it. She had planned to be up early, and go swimming with him and Bobby. She wouldn't swim, but at least she would put on her bathing suit, and make a pretense of getting wet. That was the sort of thing she planned to do all week, pretend to do everything just as always. She had failed David last night, but she would not fail him again. Her love for him would get her through the week, and her pride would stand sentinel to her weakness. It was not going to be easy, for it was hard to keep things from him. Even now, she had not fooled him into thinking she was asleep. She could feel that he was up on one elbow, looking over at her.

She tried to lie still, but the pain was there again. It gnawed through her, doubling her upwards in an arc of torture. David was at her side. He sat with her until it was morning. When he lifted the telephone to call Dr. Barry, she made no effort to stop him.

Dr. Barry came at once, carrying all his pills and medicines in his little black bag. Whenever Claudia called him for the children, it always fascinated her to see him draw from one compartment a bottle of cough medicine, from another some green capsules, from still another a box of powders. Now, however, he didn't even open his bag. He just moved his hand across Claudia's aching body and asked questions.

"There's a definite spastic condition," he mentioned briefly to David. "Nothing organic. Purely functional." He wrote out a prescription. "This will make her feel better."

"Belladonna?"

Dr. Barry nodded.

"How did you know?" Claudia asked in quick suspicion.

"Hartley's taken it for years," said David.

In spite of the belladonna, the days passed in a blur of intermittent pain. She tried to remember that David's vacation was passing too, but the pain took up all her strength and energy. She tried to smile at Bobby and Matthew, who appeared every so often and stood in the doorway, side by side like dutiful visitors. Bobby was almost two heads taller than Matthew. Whenever they stood that way, Claudia thought of a third golden head that would have completed the trio. She was always glad, when after a perfunctory exchange of talk, they drifted off again.

She no longer went through the motions of trying to get up in the morning. No one expected her to get up, with the pain breaking her body in two. Claudia heard Jane whisper to David outside her room one day, "It can't go on like this much longer. She's nothing but a bag of bones."

"I know it," David replied. "I'd hoped we could get her into town for X-rays."

"She'd never stand the trip," said Jane. "It's as much as she can do to sit up on a chair while I turn the mattress."

It was true. She had tried to hide it, but those minutes of sitting up were becoming increasingly difficult. Getting back into bed was like heaven. Going to sleep was like waking from a nightmare, for her dreams gave her the only peace she knew. Almost every night, now, she dreamed of her mother, and that she was a little girl again. Sometimes the dreams lasted over far into the next day, mingling strangely with the present.

One morning, she wakened to the sound of the lawn mower moving brusquely beneath her window. She knew before her mind was fully alive, that it was the morning of the fourteenth. She did not want to wake up to face this day, which held emptiness instead of hope. She let the sweet, nostalgic whir of the mower carry her back, back—where there was no pain and no defeat. . . . Once, when she was small, she and her mother had gone to a summer hotel, where there were wide stretches of lawn, bordered by great masses of white hydrangeas. There had been a croquet set with brightly colored stakes, and a ball with a shiny red band around it, which she had secretly chosen for her own, because it brought her luck. There was a bathhouse too, smelling damply of salt, and a small wavy mirror, and a long thin key that was apt to fall between the wide slats of the wooden floor. She couldn't have been any older than Bobby, yet suddenly she remembered that summer as vividly as if it were yesterday. More vividly, for it was hard to remember what had happened yesterday. The past seemed infinitely clearer than the present. It had more reality than the future. She had only to close her eyes and see her mother's face and be a child again. She could feel herself falling off to sleep . . . how pleasant . . . how unutterably pleasant. . . .

Bobby's shrill voice pulled at her. She could scarcely lift her heavy lids, and bring her thoughts into cohesion. It was still the fourteenth—the days were always that way, dragging out into eternity. She wanted to go back to sleep, but the raucous drone of the lawn mower scaped her nerves, and Bobby's voice went through her like a knife.

"Let me do it, Dad, I can do it!"

"No," said David. "See if mother's awake yet."

"She isn't."

"How do you know without going up?"

"Because she's always asleep," said Bobby. "Can't I just cut the front of the house?"

"The front of the house would appreciate a little weeding," said David.

Bobby was much put upon. "Can't a person even mow the lawn," he grumbled.

"No," said David. "A person can't."

A few minutes later Claudia heard Bobby pass the piano and pause to execute his one piece with much pedal and emotion. Jane's steps hurried from the kitchen. "Stop that noise, Bobby! You'll disturb your mother!"

Bobby's hands fell to the keys in a crash of despair. "Can't a person even practice!" he cried hoarsely.

"Don't answer back!" Jane reprimanded. "There's enough trouble in this house today without your misbehaving!"

Claudia thought, Jane remembers that it's the fourteenth, too. Jane had looked forward to the baby almost as much as she had.

David tiptoed to the door.

"I'm awake," she said.

He came in and sat down on the bed, and leaned over and kissed her cheek. "Bobby," he remarked, "is at the can't-a-person stage."

"I know," she said. "I heard him. 'Can't a person even practice?' " . . . The tears came. She turned her head away. "It's all my fault," she gulped. "I'm so ashamed."

"There's nothing to be ashamed of." He dried her eyes on his handkerchief. "Look," he said, "I bet you don't remember what day this is?"

So he'd remembered as well as Jane. Perhaps he

had seen the little circle marked around the date on her desk calendar. "I thought you'd forgotten," she said.

"How could I forget?" he asked her. "A week isn't very long to be with someone you love. Someone—" he spoke very slowly, "you mightn't see again for a while. . . ."

"Oh," she said. All at once she knew what he was talking about. Today was the last day of his furlough. Tomorrow morning he would go back to his post as usual. During the past week the war had faded from her immediate horizon. Even the recurring impact of his uniform had vanished, for he had worn his fatigue shirt open at the neck, and he'd looked as he had always looked. A little tired, she thought, as she noticed the lines around his mouth. He had worried about her, she could see that. She wondered whether she should tell him that it was the day the baby was to have come, and then she thought better of it.

"Funny," he went on, "you thought I'd forgotten, and I thought you'd forgotten."

She hated this new lie that lay between them, but it was better than hurting him with the truth. There seemed to be a wall between her and everything that was normal and real. A wall separated her from the children, from the sweet honest commonplaces that she had always known. She couldn't pull herself above it or over it. She felt as if she were dying behind the secret suffocation of her fear. All her life she had known fear for others. Now she knew fear only for herself. Perhaps it had always been fear for herself taking another form, and now at last, she was meeting it face to face. The thought confused her. She pushed it away and caught at the echo of what David had said. He had said "someone you mightn't see again for a while. . . ." She forced a laugh. "Even though your furlough is over," she reminded him, "I'll see you tomorrow night. It's a date."

He shook his head. "No, you won't."

"Why not?"

"Because I'm going away."

"David, where?" she cried. "For how long?"

"You never will learn to ask one question at a time, will you?"

"David," she implored. "Tell me. Where are you going?"

He hesitated. "To Washington. For a short time."

She went limp with relief. "I could wring your neck," she exclaimed. "Not that Washington's not bad enough, but for a moment I thought you might be going to be transferred—"

"Suppose I were? We'd have to live through it," he said.

"Of course," she agreed. "Only it would be a nuisance with Bobby's schooling, and running two places, and all the rest of it."

"I see," he said, with a wry smile. "You'd expect to move right along with me?"

"Certainly. That is," she amended unhappily, "if I'm ever well enough to be of any use to you."

"You'll be well," he said. "That's what I wanted to talk to you about, darling. Before I go, I'd like to know what these pains mean. I'd like another doctor, someone from New York, to see you."

"Oh David, I can't. I just can't make that trip."

"You won't have to, dear. I've asked him to come up here."

"Up here?" she echoed aghast. "It'll cost a fortune!"

"You're worth a fortune," he said. "Besides he's on his way to Boston anyway. It won't be much more than an ordinary consultation fee."

"What's his name? Is he a surgeon?"

"No. Just a diagnostician. Dr. MacGregor."

"When is he coming"

"This morning."

Her lips trembled. "That's not fair. You should have given me more time to get used to the idea."

"It was the only time he could make it. And I didn't want you to worry about it beforehand.

"I won't be operated," she said stubbornly "No matter what."

"I don't think you'll have to be. In fact I don't know what they could possibly take out."

"Gall bladder."

"What gives you that idea?"

"Miss Carey had her gall bladder taken out. It makes her mad every time she thinks of it."

"Miss Carey's a smart girl," said David. "As a matter of fact I'm having Dr. MacGregor on her recommendation. She says no one can touch him."

Claudia began swiftly to put two and two together. So David had called Miss Carey. There was only one explanation, he wanted Miss Carey to come back. How wonderful of him. She could feel herself relax against the thought. She needed Miss Carey. It would be almost as comforting as having her mother again. She wouldn't care how much pain she had, as long as Miss Carey would be there to take care of her. "This is a conspiracy," she said aloud. "You're all of you doing things behind my back. And the funny part of it is, I don't mind."

Jane was in the conspiracy, too. She had clean sheets, and Claudia's nicest nightgown and bed jacket in readiness. "If you'll please to go out, Captain Naughton," she suggested delicately, "I'll help Mrs. Naughton to change."

David absented himself with reluctance. "Why does a third person make a husband and wife feel immodest?" he objected.

Dr. MacGregor arrived a short while afterwards. He was the littlest man Claudia had ever seen. He looked particularly little beside David, and quite old. He had a very large head, and kind eyes. He gazed around, and said, "What a lovely room. It has such a peaceful feeling. The whole house has. And comfortable too. As if it had nice people living in it."

David expanded into a host. "Look at the size of these closets," he said.

Claudia thanked her lucky stars that they were tidy. Jane had tidied them only yesterday. Nevertheless, it was dangerous. She must remember to tell David not to go around showing people the inside of closets, without first making certain that they were fit to be shown.

Dr. MacGregor seemed to like the country. He stayed on and on, looking out of each window, admiring the cows in the pasture, and saying how important a farm was in wartime. "We have to keep our farms going," he said, "even if we have to use women to work them."

It was David's pet subject, and they talked about it at length. Claudia fidgeted. "Did you come to see me or the farm?" she finally asked.

Dr. MacGregor turned to her with a regretful smile. "I'm sorry. Forgive me." He sat down beside her and listened attentively while she told him how she felt. She wanted to ask him about the fall on her head, too, but it didn't seem important next to the pain in her stomach. Besides, she didn't get around to it. Before she had time to finish, he rose and took her hand. "I have to hurry along now, Mrs. Naughton. Suppose we go on with this talk some time next week in my office?"

"I couldn't possibly get to New York," said Claudia firmly. "It's as much as I can do to sit up in a chair, much less travel."

"Then we'll wait until you feel stronger," he said, pleasantly. "Good-bye, and good luck."

He was gone, before she could gather her wits. "Well, the little monkey," she observed aloud. Outrage welled up in her, followed swiftly by suspicion. Was it possible that he thought she was so ill that nothing could be done about it? Already she could hear the low professional murmur of his voice as he spoke to David in the living room. She strained to listen, but the words were unintelligible. Yet she had to know what he was saying. She got out of bed and crept to the head of the stairs.

Dr. MacGregor had stopped talking. It was David who was speaking now. "How long will she be like this?" he was asking in a muted voice.

"There's no definite prognosis," Dr. MacGregor returned. "The physical syndrome may go on for months. In cases of this sort, it may go on for years."

Everything turned black in front of Claudia's eyes. Her knees gave way, she sank to the upper step. It served her right. She shouldn't have listened. This was a cruel way of hearing one's death sentence. She had better get back to bed, and let David tell her in his own good time. But her limbs had no power in them, and the voices below continued to beat into her ears.

"Under ordinary conditions," Dr. MacGregor went on, "the length of time depends entirely upon the patient's ability to readjust herself to her environment, a re-education of the unconscious mind into an alignment with the conscious. This reluctance to face reality, is, of course, one of the underlying factors of your wife's nervous breakdown."

Nervous breakdown. The words seared into Claudia's brain like a flaming torch, and brought her to her feet with the stunning shock of it. Her mind repelled it. "No, I won't have it!" she cried out loud. "It isn't true, I won't let it be true!"

She covered her ears to shut out the words. She knew without listening, what it was all about. Dr. MacGregor was neither a physician nor a surgeon, he was a psychiatrist. She was one of hundreds, thousands, millions, whose minds were sick with the sickness that made sick bodies. The fear that was always in the back of her thoughts was coming true—Dr. MacGregor would want her to go to a sanitarium. Sanitarium. Had she imagined it or had he spoken the word? She wanted to run away from it, but she made herself stand very straight and still. She took her hands away from her ears, and listened in full awareness.

"I wouldn't say," Dr. MacGregor was continuing, "that a sanitarium as such, would be advisable under ordinary circumstances. But in view of the fact that you're leaving for foreign service so shortly, I would suggest a private nursing home, where I can watch her through the first shock of your departure. Then there's no reason why Miss Carey can't, as you suggest, continue the care of your wife at home. I have every reason to believe that as soon as she becomes resigned to your going, the environment here will be more beneficial than any other."

Claudia waited in the deathless passing of that moment, for David to speak. When he did not speak, she knew, just as surely as if she were standing beside him, that his heart was breaking.

She realized later, that in that single crushing instant of knowing that David was going overseas, her soul had been reborn. She supposed that that was the simple truth that lay behind all miracles. She did not question it at the time. Strength came to her, and she accepted it, wholly and with faith. Dr. MacGregor was only a doctor, he was not omniscient. He was wrong in saying that it might take months or years for her to emerge from darkness into light. David needed her. He needed to carry with him the thought that he was leaving her here, with his sons, in this place that they both loved. And above all, he needed her to be well. The time was short. It must happen now.

She was in the attic, finding her bathing suit, when,

finally, he came upstairs to her. She could hear him go into the bedroom.

"Claudia!"

She could hear him hurry to the bathroom, and cry out with a new panic in his voice. "Claudia! Where are you!"

She thought, regretfully, He's lost trust in me.

"I'm here!" she called to him.

She let him come up to her. Even when he saw her dressed in a pair of slacks and an old sweater, he could not believe that this was not the whim of illness. He took her hand. "Come down, dear," he said. "Come back to bed."

"David," she said, "don't be silly."

It was then that he, too, saw the miracle. It was as if, suddenly, they were stripped of bodies, and their souls emerged to meet, and touch. It was full marriage. But it was the fare of gods, and could not last. He picked her up and carried her downstairs. "You little fool," he said. "I thought you had a bellyache."

"I thought so too. It's gone. We haven't time for bellyaches. Or nervous wrecks."

He stared at her. "Claudia," he reproached her, "you listened."

"Every word," she admitted brazenly. The wall of lies was down between them. "I almost failed you, David. But I won't. I promise you."

He did not fail her either. He, too, realized that their time was short. They must live a whole life in a few short hours. All over the world, men and women were doing that. It was the price of war.

They walked out into the sunshine. Jane saw them go, and held Bobby back from following them.

"Can't a person even take a walk!" cried Bobby.

Claudia and David looked at each other and smiled. "He's a nice brat," said David.

"They're both nice brats," said Claudia. "I'll take good care of them for you."

"Don't you want to cry a little?" David asked her.

She thought about it. "I don't think so," she said. "Not now."

"Don't be ashamed if you have to."

"I won't."

"We're supposed to cry," said David simply.

She sat down on a rock, and he flung himself beside her, and laid his head in her lap.

In a little while, Jane rang the bell for luncheon. Her eyes were red. She had tried to powder them, but the powder only made them look worse. "Poor Jane," said Claudia. "She doesn't know what to make of it all."

"She hasn't been married to you as long as I have," said David.

"Are you going to eat all the time at the table now?" Bobby asked.

"Yes," said Claudia. "There'll only be the three of us, you know. You and Matthew, and I."

"Where'll Daddy be?"

David took it up from there. "I don't know. Some place exciting, though. Australia, maybe. Maybe India. Or even Africa. I'll let you know when I get there."

Bobby's eyes widened. It was the first he had heard of it. "Gosh," he said in awe. "I wish I could go too."

"You stay with mother," David said. "She'll need a man around the house."

Later, they went swimming. Claudia put her bathing suit on, and watched them from the shore. Matthew, like herself, pretended to get wet, but didn't. Bobby wanted to stay in for hours. He was full of showing off. "Watch me dive!" he yelled. "Watch how long I can stay under water!" It was little enough, thought Claudia, to give him this last hour of David.

There was just one more hour left. They spent it in their bedroom with the door closed, and Jane knowing that they wanted to be alone.

David said, "If I hadn't been sure before, darling, I'd be sure now."

"I'm sure too," she said. "So sure that I'm not afraid any longer to talk about it. But the one thing I regret is all the time I wasted."

"Don't regret it," he said. "It wasn't wasted. Every moment of it counted, every moment of it added up to now."

For an instant she fell speechless with the memory

of an agony that had no name. "It wasn't only losing the baby," she tried to make him understand, "it was losing myself—with no pathway and no light. . . ."

"I know," he said.

She looked at him in wonder. "How do you know?"

He pushed the tip of her nose lightly with his finger. "Don't ask foolish questions."

She said good-bye to him at the front gate, as she had said good-bye a thousand times in all the wonderful thousands of days of their living together. "I'm coming back," he said, "remember that."

Edward came with the car to drive him to the station. He turned his face away, while their lips met. Then David got into the car and drove away.

He had told her not to be ashamed to cry. But there would be time for tears later. Now there was work for her to do. She saw Jane sobbing at the window. She saw Bobby walk across the lawn, alone with grief. She caught up with him and put her arm around him.

"Come," she said, "let's play croquet."

He swallowed hard. "I choose red," he said.